Haunted Echoes

JULIE ANN HOWELL

the Peppertree Press
Sarasota, Florida

Graphic design by Rebecca Barbier.
Author photo on cover by Tina Parkes.
Cover illustration by Terri Bailey.

For information regarding permission,
call 941-922-2662 or contact us at our website:
www.peppertreepublishing.com or write to:
the Peppertree Press, LLC.
Attention: Publisher
1269 First Street, Suite 7
Sarasota, Florida 34236

ISBN: 978-1-936343-87-4
Library of Congress Number: 2009044018
Printed in the U.S.A.
Printed January 2010
Paperback Edition April 2011

To Sarah,

my daughter, my writing buddy …

Thank you for your honesty, encouragement to read and fix, and for your love of writing.

Chapter 1

A Stormy Night

"The sounds of the approaching storm grew closer, and the gusts of winds rattled the antiquated frame of Otter Cove Inn from attic to floor."

The lights flickered repeatedly as Sarah Reddington clicked the keyboard on her computer. She was worried that the electricity would eventually give out before nightfall. The sounds of the approaching storm grew closer, and the gusts of winds rattled the antiquated frame of Otter Cove Inn from attic to floor.

Dickens, Sarah's five-year-old yellow Lab, lay peacefully in front of the fireplace and didn't seem to be bothered by the disturbances that surrounded him.

Sarah stood up from a cozy position at her cluttered writing desk to investigate the weather and stretch her legs. She was wearing her comfy jeans, an oversized gray sweatshirt, and two different socks, as she almost always did. Of course, they never matched--one was blue argyle, and the other, solid purple. Sarah would swear that wearing two different socks was her good luck charm for writing brilliantly.

Sarah stared out the large bay window in the study, resting one knee comfortably on the cushioned seat. Her crystal blue eyes focused on the lighthouse and the bright beacon that cascaded its beam onto the deep blue waters of the Atlantic. The dark clouds were full and rolling in at a rapid pace. The setting of the lighthouse was incredible, and there was still enough daylight to make out some details of this dwelling. Its exterior dressed in patriotic colors, sitting proud and tall atop the granite cliff, with the drop below steep and immediate from the lighthouse grounds. The threatening skies in the distance overshadowed the lighthouse, giving it an eerie appearance, calling out to whoever was watching.

A cold chill ran up and down Sarah's spine, as it felt as if someone had just entered the room. Expecting to see this someone was certainly not on Sarah's mind, as she had this incredible place all to herself. Her body turned away from the ominous sky in one fell swoop as she took a rather quick inventory of the space behind her. This eighteenth-century two-story inn had many rooms within its walls, from master chambers to servants' quarters complete with a wraparound porch and a row of rustic rocking chairs. But the library was without a doubt the finest setting for inspiration and creativity. The vintage whitewashed bookcases were jam-packed with the old classics, such as *Great Expectations* and *Moby Dick*. Some of the books proved their age, disclosing tattered pages and leather-bound covers that were no longer legible. It seemed the innkeepers were sensitive to every detail of how each room was presented so vacationers would return for a long, relaxing stay year after year. A combination of a neutral palette and subtle, warm textures was used so whoever occupied the room would not be easily distracted. Old photographs in sepia tones of who appeared to be kind strangers graced the hearth of the cast-iron fireplace, each photo encased in metallic, white, and wood frames. Over the fireplace hung a turn-of-the century oil painting of a young couple and their child.

A piercing clap of thunder was all it took for the lights to give a final farewell for the night, leaving the study with its only guest and the entire inn in total darkness.

"You have got to be freaking kidding me!" said Sarah, stomping her foot on the hardwood floor.

Dickens jumped up in a ready position, sensing Sarah's frustration, and issued a low growl.

"It's okay, boy." Sarah assured him by patting him on his head a couple of times. "I am sure it is just the storm; no worries."

With only the flashes of lightning from the window and absolutely no visible flame left in the fireplace, Sarah fumbled to open the desk drawer blindly and then riffled through its contents to locate some source of illumination.

I should have been more prepared for this. What was I thinking? Sarah thought to herself.

Sarah had been independent for such a long time, she prided herself, unlike many of her girlfriends, on not spooking easily. Of course, having Dickens by her side was without doubt a plus.

"Yes, a flashlight!" After pulling her elbow in toward her body, celebrating this fine discovery, she immediately pushed the button on the side of the red plastic casing, shining the flashlight directly toward the doorway. Dickens was standing in the hallway just outside the study, his nose pointed toward the staircase, his tail down and between his legs. Her curiosity, now at its peek, sent her exploring the pitch-blackness. She made sure her steps down the hallway were cautious, but deliberate, until she reached the bottom of the majestic staircase. She placed her left hand on the smooth surface of the maple banister and pointed the flashlight straight up. The staircase had three landings, but the house itself was only two stories. The third landing stepped off and led to only one room with one door … to the attic.

A deafening slamming noise came from out of the blue directly from the floorboards above Sarah's head.

Sarah screamed at the top of her lungs and grabbed her chest.

"Holy crap! What the hell was that?" she said, still holding her chest.

This unexpected noise echoed down the staircase, conveying what sounded like a window or door opening and slamming shut, opening and slamming shut. Dickens barked just once and without hesitation bolted straight up the stairs to sniff out the noise. Sarah's heart was beating so fast she could swear a heart attack was in her immediate future. With every step she took, the noise seemed to get louder and louder, a pounding echoing deep inside the walls.

After bypassing the second story and going on to the third, she stepped off onto the landing and then up two steps. She found herself standing directly in front of the attic door, alone and in the dark. On the opposite wall from the attic was an oddly shaped stained-glass window, which hung inside the stationary window by brass chains. Although it was difficult to see, Sarah walked up to it, and with the help of the lightning from the stormy skies and her flashlight, she was able to see exactly what was happening.

The wood-frame window was swinging wildly in the breeze, crashing over and over again up against the blue clapboard siding of the inn. Sarah reached her hand through the opening so she would not knock down the stained-glass piece, the mist of the rain spraying on her face. She quickly pulled the window shut, hearing it click so it was now secure. After wiping the moisture from her face, she ran her hand along the fine-cut glass, trying to make out the intricate pattern. It was reminiscent of a family crest accented in shades of emerald greens and crimson. It was an assumption, but it appeared to be old-fashioned just like the inn.

Spinning herself around and staring once again at the attic door, she noticed it was not a traditional entrance. It appeared to be more like a storage entry, suited for a character from a fairy tale, which immediately made her think about one of the classics, *Alice in Wonderland.* Just on the edge of her vision, she noticed something was lying on the floor up against the baseboard. Still able to hear the wind whirling and whipping around the inn, she now focused on this unusually shaped object. She bent down to the floor, her knees supporting her weight, picked up the object, and laid it in the palm of her hand. Sarah shined her flashlight on this newfound treasure to find it to be just an old key. After pushing herself up from the floor, she simply tucked the key in her jeans pocket and made her way down the stairs, Dickens taking the lead, of course. As she descended down the stairs, the crystal doorknob to the attic turned slowly to the right and opened just ever so slightly.

After finding her way back to the library in the pitch darkness, wanting so desperately to write, but light challenged, she plopped down on the sofa to rest her eyes and clear her head. She was so hoping that the storm would pass and the electricity would come back on so she could work. She reached for the navy blue afghan lying on the arm of the sofa and pulled it up over her, and then immediately felt the urge to sleep almost overwhelming. The strange feeling of someone watching returned, but her eyes fell shut anyway. As she slept, the room filled with the dark shadows and soft whispers that would become all too familiar in the days to come.

Her manuscript was now calling out to her in a desperate plea to return to the world of fiction.

Chapter 2

A Writer's Routine

Sarah woke just before sunrise to the sound of the waves crashing on the rocks just below the inn. It was a hypnotic sound that was soothing to the soul. Opening her eyes and welcoming in the morning, she immediately realized her intentions of resting for just a short time the night before turned into resting until the next day.

Sitting up on the sofa, her neck stiff from sleeping in such a cramped position, she stretched her arms up above her head and immediately felt the need for a caffeine fix. Dickens was snuggled up next to her on the incredibly small space and nudged her hand, as this was a subtle hint to explore the outside.

"Okay, boy; I'm working on it," Sarah said, patting Dickens on his head.

Sarah stood up and wrapped the warm afghan around her shoulders and made her way over to the back door. It was positioned just to the left of the bay window and was an easy access to what was considered to be the backyard, the view never disappointing. The arched-shaped wooden framework was elegantly inlaid with smoky glass panels, just a few to allow the natural light to shine inside. An ivory vintage screen door was attached to the door's casing.

Dickens, at her feet, overly anxious and excited to sniff everything in sight, was scratching at the door and pacing back and forth, having no patience whatsoever for Sarah to unlock it.

"Okay, okay; hold on, you crazy dog. Give me a minute."

She barely had the screen door opened when he flew out, heading straight for the rocks. The crisp, cool air felt good on Sarah's face; she inhaled as much as she could, as if it were her first breath. Sarah, yawning and trying to wake up, watched a happy Dickens from the doorway.

The storm had passed, and everything in sight looked clean and new again. While waiting for Dickens to come back in, she turned and scanned the study and caught a glimpse of her computer, the cursor blinking in the same spot where she had stopped typing the night before, a clue that the electricity was back on. Her manuscript was now calling out to her in a desperate plea to return to the world of fiction. She was most definitely listening and willing to follow. Time to go to work!

Dickens ran back inside with just as much enthusiasm as he had going out, which meant it was time for breakfast.

The kitchen was at the back of the inn and from the study was a short walk through the dining room, down a long corridor, and then through the swinging doors.

On the way to the kitchen, Dickens took the lead, his tale hitting anything and everything that happened to get in his way.

The corridor walls were a deep indigo blue, and with the high ceilings, the white crown molding topped it off beautifully. It seemed that almost every inch of the walls was covered in gold ornate picture frames, a mix of landscapes and young families dressed in clothes not of this time period. Each face certainly could tell a story. There was one large picture that stood out more than the others. It was a portrait of a little girl; she was perhaps eight or nine years old. She was wearing a white eyelet dress and black patent leather shoes, her eyes a chocolate brown, so that when you looked real close, you could swear she was looking directly at you. Her long curly blonde hair was tied neatly with a blue ribbon. In her arms she clutched a porcelain doll dressed in the same outfit. In the left-hand corner of the painting, there was a signature and a date; the painting was simply signed "A.W. 1902."

Sarah stared at the portrait for quite some time, twirling her long auburn hair, and realized that something about the surroundings looked familiar . . . the little girl had posed for this portrait on the front porch of this inn.

The kitchen, although a small space, was adequate for preparing meals for the few guests that stayed in the inn at one given time. The farmhouse-style table appeared to have had countless coats of paint on top of its wood frame, and the ladder-back chairs were eclectic in size and color. The floor had been introduced to texture with rag rugs scattered around, which complemented everything in the room.

Sarah scooped a small amount of kibble in a bowl for Dickens, who looked up at Sarah with pure joy and anticipation. As he greedily inhaled the yummy morsels, Sarah finally had a chance to make a fresh pot of coffee. While the coffeepot gurgled and sloshed the grounds through its filter, Sarah made herself something to eat. Not much of a breakfast person, she settled for a piece of toast and thought about the annoying storm the night before. It irritated her more than anything that, because of these noises and the storm, she lost a night of writing. Perhaps this was her way of not working on her novel at all and just good old-fashioned procrastination.

After breakfast Sarah made plans with herself to jump right into her morning writing routine. When Sarah wrote her first novel, she stuck to a strict, but flexible, schedule to keep herself on task. Writing came easy for her, so it didn't matter what time of day, morning, noon, or in the middle of the night. Although "night owl" was a nickname she proudly earned in college, in fact, being a "night owl" is the only thing that got her through college. The important thing is her publisher was impressed that she came in almost three weeks under her deadline on her first book. The book, while not the biggest seller, did very well for a novice writer. Her publisher rewarded her with an awesome contract for two more books.

She had the chance to travel to Cape Elizabeth, a little town just outside of Portland, Maine, to work on the first book of her new contract.

Leaning against the kitchen counter, Sarah poured herself a cup of coffee and then flipped open her planner. Tucked inside one of the clear pockets was a recent picture of her and her publisher posing at her first book signing at Barnes & Noble, smiling one of those cheesy I-don't-want-my-picture-taken smiles, their arms linked. As she stared at the picture, it reminded her of how she ended up taking this trip to Maine.

It was a month ago, when Sarah was in the Maple Leaf office in downtown Chicago to coordinate her schedule for her upcoming book tour, sitting in a comfortable chair directly across from Anna Harrison, her publisher, when out of the blue, she suggested Sarah take a writing trip, Anna's treat. After all, Sarah had made several attempts to write her second novel, only to hit a brick wall. Her publisher suggested a change of scenery would help her creative juices to start to flow once again. But, on the other hand, she wasn't afraid to voice her opinion of hitting a brick wall or, to use the more appropriate term, writer's block. Simply put, it was crap!

Anna Harrison, a conservative businesswoman, founded the now prestigious and successful publishing house Maple Leaf. She was born and raised in the Windy City, and certainly looked the part. In her late forties, tall and slender, she had a suit in every color and always wore taupe stockings and closed-toed shoes. Her short blonde hair was tucked neatly behind her ears, and her plastic-framed reading glasses seemed to stay permanently adhered at the end of her nose regardless of whether she was using them for their purpose. One of her endearing qualities: She would talk to whomever was in the room by looking over the glasses and not through them.

Anna would go on by saying, "No one gets writer's

block, and it is just an excuse writers use when they have nothing."

She is a straight shooter and didn't pull any punches. It's not personal, just business.

Sarah didn't have to think twice about accepting Anna's offer to take this well-deserved trip and didn't bother discussing writer's block with her publisher. She figured she'd save that for another conversation as to not jinx an opportunity to get out of town.

Sarah could sense that this was going to be a great day for writing and didn't even care if she showered or not. She grabbed a notepad and pen and headed straight for the front porch, determined and ready to write, create, and get into her head, full of characters.

The weird thing she had found,
is the plotline she had intended
for this manuscript had taken a
delightful and unexpected turn.

Chapter 3

The Key

Sarah sat comfortably in the rocking chair, her pen lightly drumming the edge of her notepad. She thought to herself how effortlessly the words have been pouring out since she arrived in Maine--a far cry from the fast-paced life she led back in Chicago. It is no wonder she was having a difficult time putting her words to paper. But whatever was happening, she was completely grateful.

Well, Anna was right; the change of scenery was helpful, and in just a few days, she had written nearly one hundred pages. The weird thing she had found is the plotline she had intended for this manuscript had taken a delightful and unexpected turn.

Soaking in the salty breeze, Sarah felt something stabbing her leg. She stuck her pen behind her ear and dug into her pocket, feeling around for the source.

"Ah … my recent discovery from the third floor," she softly whispered to herself.

It was an old skeleton key, perhaps black at one time, but now a combination of both rust and green paint. She twirled it meticulously through her fingers, wondering what it opened, and then set it down on the side table next to her. She flicked it counterclockwise with her index finger, just once. Sarah watched it spin round and round, mesmerized by what was happening and looking more through it than at it, when suddenly it stopped and then flew right off the table.

She jumped straight up from the chair, dropping her notepad to the floor; it all seemed like it happened in slow motion. Although her instincts told her to run, she forced herself to walk over to the steps where it landed and try to comprehend what she had just witnessed.

"Okay, that was, well … what was that? It had to be my imagination." Dickens was by her side, panting heavily and staring at his master, waiting for her next move.

As she leaned down to search for the key, she peered through the cracks, only to see the dirt floor under the steps. Continuing her quest, she stepped down off the porch and crouched down to check it out. The key had found its resting place and was now lying motionless on the dirt floor, completely out of reach. The view under the porch certainly captured Sarah's attention. It was spectacular, any child's playground for pure joy and imagination. The porch was raised up by concrete blocks, just enough for someone to crawl under it. Taking in the sight, Sarah caught a glimpse of something sticking out of one of the blocks. Intrigued, she scooted herself over and reached her small hand inside the jagged-edged slab and pulled out a weathered envelope. It was loosely tied with a piece of brown twine. Before she had a chance to open it, she was interrupted by a very disturbed Dickens barking uncontrollably …

Sarah could sense that she was no longer alone.

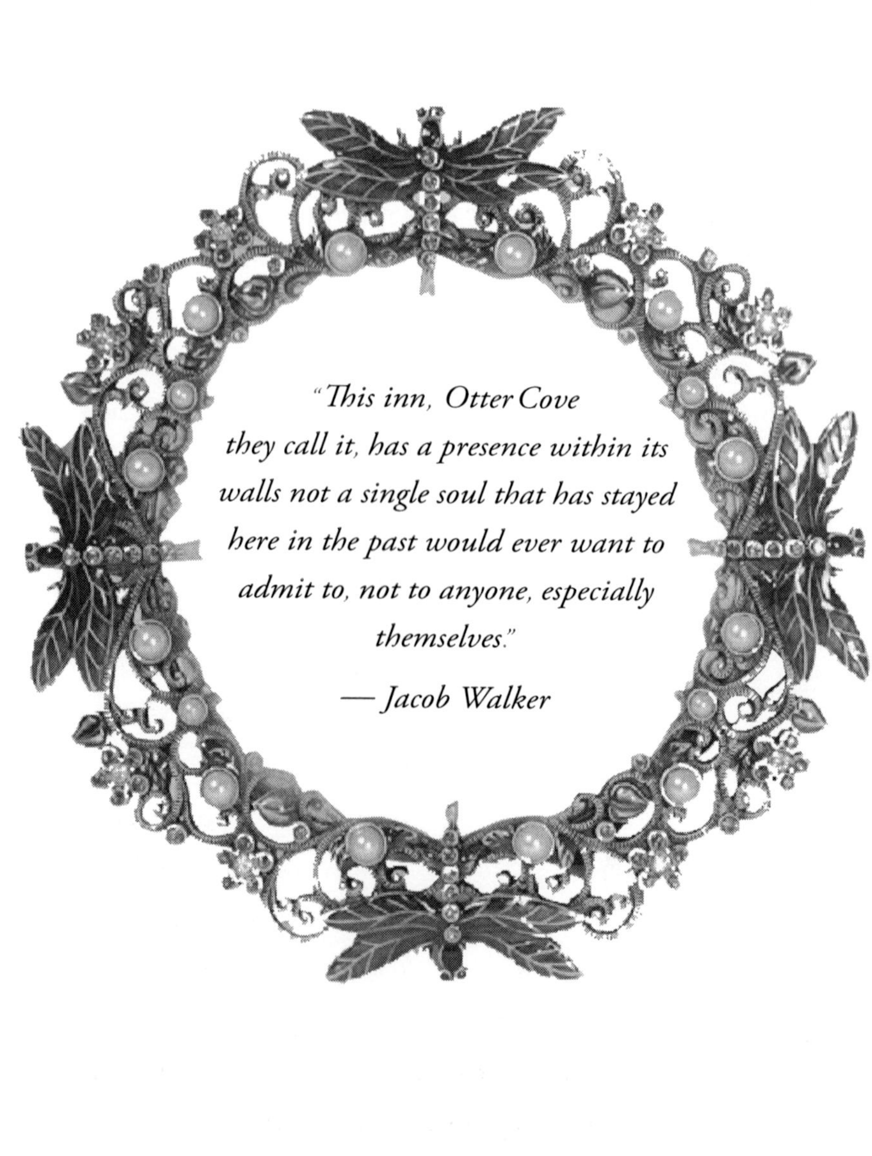

"This inn, Otter Cove they call it, has a presence within its walls not a single soul that has stayed here in the past would ever want to admit to, not to anyone, especially themselves."

— Jacob Walker

Chapter 4

The Stranger

Anxious to get out from underneath the porch, Sarah backed out clumsily on all fours, hushing Dickens on her way and determined to free herself from the tight quarters. Finally back on her two feet, she promptly stuffed the envelope in her pocket. She wiped her hands off on the front of her jeans and was now focused on the stranger standing on the walkway.

Shielding her eyes from the glare of the sun, she was able to size him up in no time. He was a tall man, slender built, dressed in a grungy gray T-shirt, baggy jeans, and black boots. The deep lines on his face not only gave away his age, but also were a dead giveaway that he was a serious smoker.

"Can I help you?" Sarah said, securing a hold on Dickens' blue leather collar, and then she softly commanded him to stay. Dickens let out a low growl, sat down, and glared intently at the intruder.

There was no response to this simple question, only uncomfortable silence. The stranger's eyes were a dull brown, and it appeared that the life inside them had vanished. His stare gave Sarah chills.

"Well, I am waiting," Sarah said, putting her hands in her pockets and swaying her body from side to side, a nervous habit to calm her nerves.

"You know this place is haunted?" the stranger blurted out without hesitation or an introduction. This blunt delivery left Sarah speechless and waiting for him to utter his next word.

After taking out a crumpled pack of Camels from his breast pocket, he casually slid one out and into his mouth, finding that familiar resting spot.

He patted his pockets, mumbling something to himself, and then pulled out a red lighter from the plastic sleeve of the pack and lit his cigarette.

"This inn--Otter Cove, they call it--has a presence within its walls not a single soul that has stayed here in the past would ever want to admit to, not to anyone, especially himself. And the ground we stand on--it's surrounded by evil."

He took a long drag of his cigarette and turned his head to the side, exhaling the white smoke slowly through his nose and mouth, his front teeth yellow and decayed.

He went on with his story.... "The authorities found two dead bodies on the second floor. Of course, it made the front-page news of *The Beacon Journal;* the entire town talked about it for quite some time. A man and woman were found dead on the second floor of this inn. Their necks were broken, and their bodies were twisted in such a way that no person could explain it. The private investigators never did find the killer or the murder weapon."

"Killer," Sarah interrupted.

"That's what I said--killer, a cold-blooded murderer." His speech was slurring at this point. "That very same day the authorities found the two dead bodies, the lighthouse keeper witnessed a little girl running from this old inn toward the rocks. She was screaming hysterically and carrying on. He called out to her; she kept running, looking back toward the inn and then toward the water. She lost her balance on the rocks and fell to her death, or so it seemed. But when the lighthouse keeper ran over to the cliff's edge, she was nowhere to be found. The town locals have said that this little girl was involved somehow, that she was the daughter of the couple that were found dead inside this inn. She has been seen by many people, a spirit lost and now searching for answers. Didn't anyone tell you?"

"Well, actually, no, of course not. I have not seen or spoken to anyone to tell me anything. However, I would be interested to know how you found out that I was staying here. I would also like to know your name since you have failed miserably to mention it even once during this little chat we've been having."

The tone is Sarah's voice intensified, and now this stranger could sense an introduction would be a good idea.

"My apologies for being so direct, miss; habit of mine to just run my mouth. My name is Jacob. Jacob Walker."

Sarah leaned in to extend her hand to shake his, but he took a step back, tucking his hands in his jean pockets. He offered no explanation, just continued his introduction.

"As I was saying, I am one of the local fishermen here in Cape Elizabeth. Been here now, well, seems like a hundred years, and I suppose it has been. I heard a rumor that a young woman was staying here, so I took the ferry over to warn you about something."

"Warn me about what, Mr. Walker?" Sarah said.

"I wanted to explain about the murders and how not a soul will set one foot inside this old place. It was abandoned by the last owners and left here to rot.

"Have you seen her?" Jacob said, shifting his body weight to the other hip and glancing around Sarah as if he was looking for something.

"Seen whom?" Sarah said.

"The little girl."

Before Sarah could respond, the stranger continued his description of the little girl.

"She skips along the rocks, humming an eerie tune--no words, just a soft hum. She clutches something in her arms that no one has been able to make out. Some say that they have seen a shadow of what appears to be a little girl in the attic window of this inn. Have you heard anything strange coming from the third floor, miss?"

"Tell me, Mr. Walker, how do you know so much about this little girl?"

"I believe she is my granddaughter."

Her emotions just swept over her
as she would now read
the words she anticipated
from the past.

Chapter 5

Past Voices

Sarah watched the mysterious stranger walk away from the inn and disappear down the pathway. Confused more than ever, she decided to put their creepy conversation on hold and open the envelope she found under the porch.

Sitting on the front steps of the inn, she pulled it out of her back pocket and studied it for just a brief moment. Untying the brown twine and opening the flap, she took a deep breath, not really knowing what to expect. Her emotions just swept over her, as she would now read the words she anticipated from the past.

The writing appeared to be feminine, in longhand; the now faded black ink was barely legible on the yellowed, stained stationery. Sarah decided to read it out loud, slowly and articulately, so conceivably each word would show her the way to answers … the answers to so many questions.

Dear Lily Rose,

Oh, sweet girl, I am so sorry I could not come and get you. I hope you are safe hiding in one of the rooms. I tried to find you, but it found me first, so I ran. Your dolly will protect you, I promise. I am in the attic hiding from the monster that is chasing me. I don't think I have ever been so frightened in my life. I don't have much time. I found this parchment in the attic trunk and wanted so desperately to write to you, one last letter. I can feel his presence getting closer and closer; there is nothing that I can do now. I think your father is gone. We were running up the stairs together, and somehow, somehow, my love, it took him; the monster took him away. It is too late for your father and for me, but not for you, my love.

The pounding is getting louder and louder. It's here. Pray for me, as it will soon be over. I beg you, my love, find out what did this to us…. Search for the answers…. Look for the key; it opens the trunk in the attic…. The answers are there. The answers are in the music....

Good-bye, my love.
Your loving mother,
C.W.

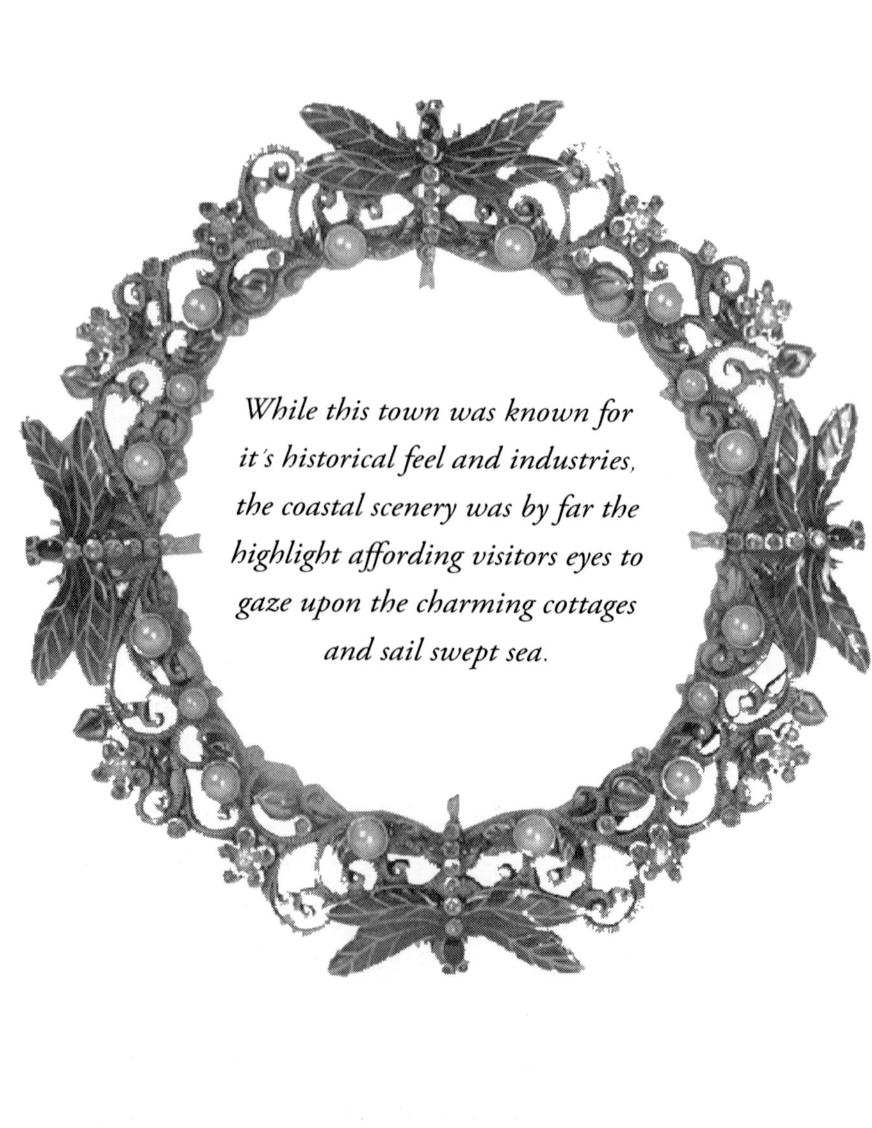

While this town was known for it's historical feel and industries, the coastal scenery was by far the highlight affording visitors eyes to gaze upon the charming cottages and sail swept sea.

Chapter 6

Missing Pieces

Sarah was losing her capacity to think clearly, as the events of the inn had now gone way beyond comprehensible, to say the least. Just in the past few days, during this peaceful visit to the inn, she has encountered more than she bargained for. This was supposed to be a writing excursion, not a ghost hunt. But something or someone was pushing her to find the answers to the many lost questions and to keep searching.

Was The Otter Cove Inn left abandoned with everything in its place, down to the fine china and stemware? Although she was totally clueless when she arrived and didn't pay any attention to it (Why would she?), the door was unlocked, and the key was just sitting there on the kitchen table--no note, no instructions. Where were the innkeepers? Why were they not there to greet her? Who murdered the couple found on the second floor? Who was this Jacob Walker, and was he even telling her the truth?

Sarah decided to get an early start on a new day and head into town. She took a hot shower and washed her long, straight hair. Getting dressed was the easy part, as her wardrobe consisted of mostly jeans, tanks, and flip-flops. As she was choosing for the day's outfit, the blue and white tank combined with her Chicago Bears sweatshirt tied around her waist was the ticket. Her satchel-style purse topped it off, crossing her chest, leaving her hands free. Her hair still wet, she brushed it back and tied it in a ponytail with a black scrunchy.

She grabbed her keys from the entry table, and Dickens wagged his tail, thinking for sure that he was going too.

"Not this time, boy; stay here and keep your wet nose to the ground in search of ghostly visitors, okay, buddy?"

As she drove down Old Ocean House Road, following the road signs toward town, her elbow leaning on the driver's door and her hand rubbing her left temple, she was trying to put the puzzle together, but there were so many pieces missing.

It seemed ironic that her rental car was a Ford Focus. That was something she should have been doing--focusing on her writing--but instead, she had assigned herself to a full-fledged murder investigation.

As she was in deep thought, her cell phone sang out. Digging in her suitcase of a purse, holding the wheel with one hand, she managed to turn the corner while searching for her phone, which was playing that annoying ringtone by Fergie, "Big Girls Don't Cry." How appropriate. Looking at the screen, realizing who it was …, "Crap, it's my publisher. Sorry, but this is so not the time to have a chat with 'all business Anna,'" she blurted out loud. Sarah pressed the ignore button and tossed her phone back in her bag.

The small town of Cape Elizabeth was just that, small. It was just a hop, skip, and a jump from Portland and marked the entrance to Casco Bay. There were only three principal roads that all led to the heart of the antiquated town, with a population at the moment of 9,068. A green and blue sign with clip art of a lighthouse plunked under the words sits, well, more like leans in the grass along the side of the road. The population number is written in chalk so it could be altered at the appointed time by applying simple addition and subtraction. It was a true and genuine welcome for any and all who come for a visit.

While this town was known for its historical feel and industries, the coastal scenery was by far the highlight, affording visitors eyes to gaze upon the charming cottages and sail-swept sea. It didn't matter where you were standing; all eyes were able to appreciate the strategically placed buildings along the coastline, which were better known as the beacons of light--you guessed it, the lighthouses. They were among the main attractions in Maine and the biggest moneymaker, which brought well-deserved tourism dollars to the hardworking residents.

Sarah parallel parked her small compact car along the main drag, appropriately named Main Street U.S.A. *How cliché*, she thought to herself. The stores and restaurants, from a barbershop to a candy store, were all lined up. It looked as if she had just stepped onto the set of "The Andy Griffith Show."

Being that this was Sarah's first trip into town, she felt a little awkward and out of place. The whispering and pointing of fingers behind her back did not go unnoticed.

Choosing a random stranger on the sidewalk, she prepared to fire away her first question as a private investigator.

"Excuse me, sir, can you point me in the right direction of where I might find the daily newspaper building?"

The nameless resident stopped in his tracks, facing Sarah, let out an annoying sigh, pointed in the proper direction--no words, not even a hello, and then just moved along the sidewalk.

"Well, thank you ever so much. I appreciate your time, and do have a nice day," Sarah said sarcastically, shouting out in frustration to the appointed stranger, who was walking briskly down the sidewalk. He never glanced back at Sarah, not once.

The entrance to the old brick building was a simple design with an assortment of brass and glass furniture. The almond-colored walls had a wooden chair rail painted hunter green. There were three curio cabinets side by side, filled with an array of memorabilia and award plaques given to the journalists past and present. On the walls were poorly framed archives of important headlines of front-page news of what was called *The Cape Courier*. There didn't seem to be any sign or hint of a paper called *The Beacon Journal*, as Jacob Walker had mentioned.

The young girl behind the circular desk was filing her acrylic nails and chewing gum, smacking and popping it so loud that the sound bounced off the walls, filling the once silent space with an extremely annoying vibration.

Sarah cleared her throat just once, as to try to get her attention.

The young girl looked up and said, "Yeah, what can I do for you?"

"Hi. I was wondering how I might go about viewing

some past issues of the paper, and I am also just a little curious, did the name of this paper used to be *The Beacon Journal*?"

"I have no idea, lady. I just work here." After stretching her purple bubble gum out of her mouth and then placing it back in again, she hastily rattled off the following instructions.

"To find the archives, walk down this hallway to my left, stop at the elevator doors, push the elevator button, step inside, then press the button that has the number four on it. Once you arrive on the fourth floor, step off, and you will find all the old papers you need to read from long ago to present day. Is that clear?"

The young lady immediately went back to filing her nails and chewing her purple bubble gum.

"Yes, perfectly clear. Sounds great. I will do just that. Thanks," Sarah said, tapping her hand twice on the Formica countertop.

Sarah smashed the elevator button for "up" and mumbled, "Smart ass" under her breath loud enough for the "smart ass" to actually hear. "Wow, so far everyone is just so accommodating here in Cape Elizabeth," Sarah said, and she rolled her eyes as the door shut.

The rickety elevator made its way up the shaft and stopped on floor number four, as instructed. The cables bounced the steel box a couple of times before it settled itself. The doors opened, and a cold breeze hit Sarah right in the face. Floor number four had no sign of anyone at work; it was dead silent. The only light was coming from the dingy windowpanes at the back of the room. There were stacks and stacks of boxes filled with newspapers piled all the way to the ceiling. There were crumpled-up, disjointed pages sort of floating along the floor like Texas tumbleweeds. Sarah stood astonished, staring at the disarray of black-and-white current events, not only taken aback at the way they were stored, but confused about where to begin.

"Well, I suppose the old saying is true: Be careful what you wish for," Sarah said out loud, her voice echoing off the walls.

Sarah decided to make herself at home, kicked off her shoes, and sat herself down on the floor and crossed her legs. The light from the windows shone in the exact spot necessary, so she was able to see the disorganized chaos. She found herself getting swallowed up in the now forgotten stories from the past, reading each word carefully as not to miss any details. Each story was the typical small town news, from a family cat stuck in a tree, to the football players from the high school destroying school property just for the hell of it. There wasn't anything unusual or earth-shattering, but she was determined to find a clue that would intrigue her interest. Just at that moment, a section of one of the papers drifted slowly down from the top of the pile and landed right in Sarah's lap. It was as if someone just handed it to her to read. The headlines screamed off the page in big, bold letters, "Local Fisherman Jacob Walker Drowns in Tragic Boating Accident." The newspaper she was holding: *The Beacon Journal.* The date: September 23rd, 1826.

She was not alone,
there was a presence right next
to her, and it was getting
stronger by the minute.

Chapter 7

Beyond the Grave

The fourth floor of *The Cape Courier* building had an eerie quiet within its red brick walls, leaving only one soul sitting alone on the cold linoleum floor. Sarah was surrounded by pages of tabloid news and advertisements, with just one paper of interest in her hand of an archaic journal dated over two hundred years ago, the shock on her face of having just read the odd story of Jacob Walker drowning in a boating accident. That was the same stranger that exchanged words with her the day before. The man in the photo below the antiquated headlines was standing on the dock, holding a prize-winning fish and posing for the camera. He had on a gray T-shirt, baggy jeans, and black boots, and a cigarette was hanging out of his mouth. This man was undeniably Mr. Walker, dressed in the exact same clothes that he was wearing the day they met. She recalled, when he introduced himself, he had mentioned that he was a local fisherman and had lived in Cape Elizabeth for many years. Did she dream it? Was she imagining the entire conversation? Was he a supposed spirit with an unsettling past, only trying to reach out in hopes of finding his granddaughter? It was an unsolved mystery from beyond the grave.

The elevator gears abruptly switched themselves on, making a grating noise, and the elevator made its slow climb back up the shaft from the ground level. Someone was on the way up to give Sarah fair warning that the newspaper was about to close for the day. The time had sailed by, and realizing now after looking at her silver watch, it was already five o'clock. Without even thinking, she stuffed the journal inside her tan canvas satchel and headed for the elevator doors. Pacing back and forth and feeling just a little panicked, she smashed the down button a few more times, as if this would somehow speed it along.

"Come on, already; I want to get the hell out of here!" she said with frustration. She stared up at the numbers, watching intently as each floor had its turn to shine. She readied herself to once again meet face to face with the gum-chewing girl who so graciously greeted her when she arrived that morning. She was almost certain she would be inside the steel compartment, ready to give her the news that her investigation period was up and she needed to vacate the building immediately. The elevator seemed to take an eternity to reach its destination, and when it finally did, the doors opened sluggishly, as if it were teasing and taunting her, but come to find out, there was nobody inside. Sarah cautiously moved forward, turned around, and then pushed the "lobby" button to go down. The space in the elevator didn't feel right. It was different, as if all the oxygen had been sucked out somehow. She wasn't alone; there was a presence right next to her, and it was getting stronger by the minute. Tapping her foot on the floor, her patience wearing down at this point, she felt creeped out and overly anxious to get out of the building as soon as possible. But something was tugging at her pant leg; something was most definitely touching her clothing. Sarah backed herself in the corner of the elevator and screamed as loud as she could, "What do you want? Who is here with me? What do you want?"

A childlike voice engulfed the air and whispered these simple words: "Help me."

She was not sure what to think and her mind was racing as well as her heart as this was an experience that she had never encountered before.

Chapter 8

A Trusted Friend

Sarah jumped into her car, slinging her bag across the passenger seat, her hands shaking uncontrollably, trying to insert the key in the ignition. She was not sure what to think, and her mind was racing as well as her heart, as this was an experience that she had never encountered before. She found herself driving back toward the inn, but needed to collect herself, calm down, and get some food and a cup of coffee. She remembered passing by a quaint restaurant on the way into town that morning, just off State Road 77. The restaurant was on the opposite side of the entrance to the lookout at Kettle Cove and the state park, no more than ten minutes from downtown.

The sunset in the horizon left behind a painted sky of oranges, reds, and pinks. It was so beautiful and rather peaceful. Although Sarah was not feeling so peaceful at the moment, she had to tell someone about what she had just experienced, but who would believe this bizarre story? Most would think she was out of her mind and just making it up. After all, she is a novelist; fiction is her life. The only person in the world that would listen to this outrageous ghost story and not judge or make fun was her best friend and book editor, Charlotte Dawson.

The phone rang a couple of times, and on the other end was a welcoming and familiar voice.

"Hey, stranger, how are things going for you? Are you busy working on your new book? You must be so excited," Charlotte said, with her usual spin on enthusiasm.

"Hi, Charlotte. Things are going great. Anna most likely mentioned that I am hiding out, tucked far away between all of the beautiful lighthouses of Maine. I am calling, as I needed to hear a friendly voice, your voice," Sarah said, but not too convincingly, which was apparent.

"Yes, Anna did mention it in passing, but what's wrong, kiddo? You don't sound like yourself. Talk to me!"

Charlotte was only ten years older than Sarah, and yet they had so much in common. Charlotte had been the editor-at-large at Maple Leaf for five years now, and she and Sarah became fast friends after her first edit as a novice writer. When Anna signed Sarah's second book, Charlotte was over-the-top proud and excited to be able to work alongside Sarah once again on another book project, more so than Anna, or so it seemed. Charlotte was so easy to work with and to talk with no matter the circumstances and pretty much the only one she could entrust with her written words.

"Charlotte, I am at a stopping point right now on my novel--not by choice, believe me. My research has ceased for my novel and has been involuntarily redirected toward the bizarre happenings that have been occurring since I arrived in Maine."

"What sort of bizarre happenings?" Charlotte asked, intrigued.

"Let's see, where to begin? I am hearing noises, seeing objects move right before my eyes, talking to strangers who just so happen to be dead." Sarah stopped herself, realizing that it sounded even more ridiculous to say it out loud.

Charlotte waited for just a moment and then said with the utmost confidence, "Well, if I know my best friend, you are checking into it, right? You weren't a journalist for all those years for nothing, you know? You are not just sitting back and letting it all happen; you are doing something about it, right?"

"Yes, of course; my skills just kicked in almost like clockwork. You know me by now. In fact, I am driving back from downtown Cape Elizabeth right now. I have spent the entire day searching the archives of the daily newspaper, the only newspaper in this old town. I even managed to borrow a few papers that I didn't have time to read, so I could read them later when I get back to the inn. Wait, Charlotte; before you say anything, I know what you are thinking. No worries. I will return them, I promise."

Charlotte laughed, "Of course, I know you will return the papers. I wasn't going to say anything about that, I swear. So, let's move on, shall we?"

"What is the name of the inn that Anna hooked you up with? I forgot," Charlotte said, riffling through her desk full of edits and file folders in search of a pen so she could write it down. "Okay, got a pen; shoot."

"It's called The Otter Cove, one of the oldest inns here in Maine. Charlotte, it is so beautiful. You would love it. The inn sits high up on a cliff with a picturesque view of the ocean and a lighthouse. It is almost as if you are looking right at an oil painting--absolutely gorgeous. And this has been my view every day for the past several weeks; it is honest to goodness any writer's dream escape to create without interruptions. You can look it up online if you want to check it out."

"Wow! It sounds amazing."

"Come to find out, I am the only person registered, or maybe not. It's hard to say." With that said, Sarah smiled just a little, as she was already feeling better.

"Did I sense a little relief just now?" Charlotte asked.

"Well, yes, I suppose you did at that; thank you for cheering me up and listening to this incredulous anecdote, although it's not just an anecdote. I am positive that I didn't imagine all of this. I need you to believe me. You do believe me, right?" Sarah said with a desperate plea in her voice.

"Of course, I have no reason to not believe you. What are you going to do next?" Charlotte asked.

Sarah let out a much-needed sigh. "Well, I need to keep digging and searching, especially for the history of the inn. I need to find out who the mysterious couple were that were murdered inside the inn, the couple that Jacob Walker told me about. I am also curious why the innkeepers weren't here to welcome me when I arrived. Then I have the issue with Jacob Walker, the dead fisherman that showed up on my walkway out of nowhere. That is a mystery in itself to solve. I certainly didn't want to bother Anna about this, as I don't want to seem ungrateful and disappointed in the accommodations she has set me up with for this writing excursion. She already thinks most of her writers are completely insane." Sarah so knew that Charlotte would say something brilliant about now to make her feel better.

"I would have to agree with you on that one; most of the writers we publish are just a little bit on the crazy side, excluding you, of course."

"Yes, of course. That's what you say to me now, but I am sure you have a much different story to tell to those behind my back." Sarah laughed softly.

"Now, I am not sure what to tell you about the fisherman character, but if you said you saw him and spoke with this man, then you must have. I will do some checking on this end and see what I come up with. Do you want me to come and stay with you? I am sure I would be able to get away for a few days," Charlotte said politely.

"No, Charlotte. You have way too much to do. Really, I will be just fine. No worries, but thank you for offering."

"Okay, well, I do have to scoot, as I am on deadline to finalize an edit for an author, and if I don't finish soon, he will have my head. I must say he does not get to press the easy button."

They had a great laugh and said their good-byes.

The walls were an open scrapbook of an authentic collection of letters, pressed stationery, and vintage postcards held up by rusty pushpins.

Chapter 9

Table for One

The Good Table Restaurant had a serene spirit about it and felt like coming home the moment Sarah pulled in the crowded parking lot. The soft butter yellow and white cottage-style dwelling was reminiscent of a simpler lifestyle. The small hand-painted sign attached to the wooden post read "Honest Food and Honest Prices," which definitely gave it that mom-and-pop feel.

There were a few groups of people waiting to be seated, rocking by the time in oversized swings lined up on the front porch. Sarah breezed right by them, and a gentleman graciously held the door as she made her way into the parlor. The smell of warm apple pie and freshly brewed coffee was in the air. The one-room restaurant was distinctive and old-world. Surrounding the perimeter were wooden shelves with nostalgic boxes designed from old candy containers. The walls were an open scrapbook of an authentic collection of letters, pressed stationery, and vintage postcards, held up by rusty pushpins.

Still taking it all in, Sarah gave her name right away to the hostess, who asked politely, "How many in your party?"

"Table for one, please."

No waiting for Sarah; the hostess said with a smile, "Right this way."

She followed the young, slender girl over to the window and sat in a small, cozy two-seat booth. It was the perfect amount of space for her, her many notes, and a cup of coffee that was delivered to her without her even asking. The ceiling fan was blowing right on her, so she untied her sweatshirt from her waist and pulled it over her skimpy tank top. To get a feel for the place, she scanned the room, and everyone was engrossed in deep conversation and enjoying what seemed to be, by and large, the catch of the day. She took a peek at the menu, and with great satisfaction and relief to find that grilled chicken, homemade soup, and salad made the cut. They were always her first choice--never fish, not ever.

The server took her order, and she sipped her coffee,

staring out into the parking lot, sort of registering the day's events. It felt so good to be out in the real world, in a manner of speaking, with what appeared to be normal people, doing normal things.

As she turned back, her eyes met another's. He was staring directly at her. His sudden stare made her feel uncomfortable, to some extent, embarrassed. She even turned around to see if he was, in fact, looking at her and no one else. He was sitting at the counter, inhaling a sandwich, grinning at Sarah, and attempting to wipe the mayo off his handsome chin all at the same time. It was almost comical to watch and charming at the same time. He was in his mid-thirties and had unforgettable gorgeous green eyes. It was difficult to tell how tall he was because he was sitting on the edge of the barstool. His hair was shaved close to his scalp, not because he was going bald, but just because he could. His uniform was a dead giveaway to what he did for a living. He was wearing a crisp pair of khaki pants and a navy blue camp shirt. The triangular patch on the sleeve was embroidered with the words "Scotts Dale Police Department." The officer kept fidgeting with his radio, adjusting the volume so as to not disturb anyone sitting nearby. Most could hear the garbled calls coming through anyway, but all were nonsense. It was obvious that he was on his dinner break and didn't have much time left the way he was gulping down his food. He slapped a twenty down on top of the ticket and signaled to his server he was done, all the while still keeping a close eye on Sarah's table.

Sarah felt her body shrinking down in the seat. "Oh, crap. He is coming over here. Act natural. Don't be an idiot," she whispered to herself.

Sarah pretended to be busy writing when the police officer slid into the seat opposite hers and then asked straight out, "So, you are a Chicago Bears fan, I see?"

"What gave it away?" Sarah said, just like a true smart ass. Returning a question to avoid answering one was her favorite thing to do, no matter the circumstance. Seemed to be some sort of defense mechanism she had conjured up when it came to communicating with handsome men.

"Well, I believe your sweatshirt was my first hint--unless it's not yours and belongs to your boyfriend or husband maybe?" He folded his arms and waited for her next thought.

"Is that your way of flirting with me, officer_____?"

"Storms. Riley Storms. And you are?"

"Reddington. Sarah Reddington."

"Wow, again with the smart ass stuff. That must get exhausting for you after a while." His delightful smile made her squirm just a little. She was feeling optimistic and hopeful he didn't notice.

"I will never tell," Sarah said, blushing at this point, still loving the game she was playing.

"So, I take it that you are a writer, Sarah Reddington."

"Why, because I am sitting in a booth alone, writing? Aw, you caught me; now you know all about me."

His piercing green eyes stared right into hers, and she could tell at this point, he was getting somewhat annoyed at the game she was playing. He seemed genuinely interested in getting to know Sarah Reddington, the Bears fan/writer.

"Okay, I will be straight with you," Sarah said with a smirk.

"I really haven't been out much lately, and the only one that I have to talk to is my dog, Dickens. He doesn't have too much to say; he just listens, which is a good thing if you are a writer and really don't want an honest opinion. His is always a five-star rating. Sorry, I am babbling as usual. To answer your question, yes, you are correct, I am a writer, a published one at that and now working on my second novel."

"Is that right. Anything that I might have seen on the shelves?" He sat up a little taller, waiting in anticipation to hear her blurt out a recognizable book title.

Their conversation was briefly interrupted as the server plunked the tan wicker basket in front of her with her food neatly arranged inside. It was perfect timing, her saving grace from not having to give out the not-so-popular book title published last year.

"Hope you don't mind if I eat, Officer Storms; it has been a long day, and I am famished." Sarah placed her napkin on her lap and started right in on her sandwich.

"No, please go ahead. I have to run in just a few minutes anyway, but please call me Riley." His eyes filled with more questions, as he pondered to himself, *Do I ask or not?* He went for it.

"So where do writers like you go to write? Do you have a quiet place here in Cape Elizabeth to work, or do you prefer chaos and conversation all around you?"

After taking a sip of her cold coffee, Sarah smoothed out her napkin on her lap, a nervous twitch to bide her time to come up with something to say.

"Those are a couple of interesting questions, as I figured you already knew the answer to at least where I was staying, since this town is so incredibly small."

"You know, you are so right. News does travel fast around here, but I haven't heard anything about you, and believe me, I would have remembered. But if I were a writer, and by all means, I am not, my first guess would be that you are staying at a B and B--am I right?" The officer sat there, looking all sure of himself.

"What makes you say that, officer?"

"I suppose you could say you have that big city look about you, and I certainly don't picture you staying at a Motel 6."

"Yep, you are absolutely on the money; I am staying at a bed-and-breakfast just a few miles from here, on the hill."

Still enjoying her dinner, she didn't pay any attention to Officer Storm's reaction.

"You mean The Otter Cove Inn?" Riley asked, the pitch in his voice rising.

"Yes, I believe that is the name of the inn. That's the one. And may I ask, why do you have such a horrific look on your face? You are freaking me out. Is there something I should know about Otter Cove?" Sarah started fidgeting with her bag at this point in search of her car keys.

"No, no; it's nothing, really. But are you sure the name of the inn where you are staying is the Otter Cove? The reason I am asking that question is it was my understanding that Otter Cove Inn was shut down a long time ago, even condemned." He folded his strong arms, waiting for her response.

"Well, you are mistaken because the door was wide open, and I have been staying there for a few weeks now." Sarah finally located her keys and set them next to her bag just in case she needed to make a quick getaway.

"Okay, I suppose I could be wrong. I have been wrong

before, or so they tell me."

The two of them sat quiet for what seemed like an eternity, until the officer broke the awkward silence.

"Well, since you are staying at the inn on the hill, you must have met the lighthouse keeper," Riley said.

"No. I have wanted to take a walk down to the lighthouse, but just haven't taken the time yet."

"You should go introduce yourself. He is quite the character."

"Maybe I will."

"Well, it was nice meeting you," the officer said, scooting out of the booth and extending his hand, all the while still talking.

Sarah wiped her hands on her napkin and shook his hand.

"It was nice to meet you as well, and let me just say thank you; you are the first person that has actually been nice to me other than the hostess that sat me here in this cozy space." Sarah was now looking up at the officer standing next to her.

"Really--how is that possible when Cape Elizabeth is known for its down-to-earth appeal and hospitality? You must be hanging with the wrong crowd. Maybe I'll see you around town." He smiled and walked toward the front door, giving a salute to the owner, behind the counter, before he left.

Sarah watched the handsome officer walk across the parking lot to his squad car. It was a coincidence perhaps that his car was parked next to hers. Grabbing ahold of the silver handle, he hesitated for a moment and then glanced up at Sarah, who was still sitting in the window seat, catching her staring at him as well. There was something about the way he looked at her this time. A writer, an observer, she could sense that he knew more than he wanted to share about the town, the inn, the people in Cape Elizabeth. It seemed obvious to her that he was holding on to a secret about what really happened in the old inn so long ago. Maybe he wanted to tell her about the murders, or warn her about the ghosts that now wander the hallways, casting shadowy figures on the walls and searching themselves for what was once a reality. She could see that he was hiding something from her; the truth was in his eyes.

The branches reached straight out like fingers, casting an eerie shadow on the blue clapboard siding.

Chapter 10

The Music Box

The crunching sound coming from the car tires was deliberate, like footsteps walking heavily over rock and shell. The tires were spitting, sputtering small pieces up under the steel rims until the car came to its final resting spot. Although the ignition was turned off, the engine was still clicking and dripping in an attempt to cool itself down from the day's drive. Sarah was glued to the blue upholstered seat, hesitant to get out of the car for the many reasons that still cannot be explained.

Pressing her chest up against the black leather steering wheel, she was stretching every muscle in her body to see the old house out of the front windshield, as if it were the first time. There had to be something she was missing, and perhaps it had been right in front of her face the entire time.

The inn was pitch-dark inside and out and sitting there in complete solitude. The grand, stately oak trees that encircled the property were standing tall, swaying back and forth in the cool night breeze. The branches reached straight out like fingers, casting an eerie shadow on the blue clapboard siding. Sarah knew eventually that she had to walk through the front door, as her responsibilities were waiting for her--Dickens, her novel. Everyone was depending on her to hand over finished pages, ready for print, ready to be in the hands of her readers. She finally convinced herself to get out of the car.

Sarah twisted the brass handle and pushed the door open, sending it crashing up against the maple paneling, not realizing her own strength. Standing in the foyer, she was expecting to be happily greeted by a famished Dickens, but he was nowhere in sight. The foyer, although a small space, would take anyone's breath away, as the overstated twelve-foot ceilings gave it that opulent feel. The exquisite paneling covered the walls from ceiling to floor. The only piece of furniture: an antique hall tree decorated with stylish velvet hats, each hanging on individual hooks.

Sarah turned on the light, hung her satchel on the hall

tree alongside the hats, and dropped her car keys in the pocket. Curious where Dickens was hiding out, she tilted her head and concentrated intently on the characteristic noises the old inn made, as she had grown quite accustomed to them in the past few weeks. Oddly enough, the inn wasn't making any noises whatsoever; everything was still, as if the inn had stopped breathing. Sarah gave herself a hug, as it suddenly felt colder inside than it did outside. She rubbed her arms in an attempt to warm herself up, all the while calling out for Dickens. She then whistled a couple of times, but still nothing.

Resting her hands on the banister and listening closely for any sign of her four-legged friend, this time, she heard a faint noise. It was music, soft music, and it was coming from one of the rooms upstairs, echoing through the floor vents down to the ground level. The tune was not recognizable, but it was playful, melodic, and mechanical.

As she moved up the flight of stairs, the floorboards under her feet complaining, creaking, and aching with each step, the volume of the musical notes intensified the higher she climbed.

There were eight guest rooms, all to be found on the second floor overlooking the Atlantic Ocean. The heavy maple doors had crystal knobs and a silver plate placed strategically in the center of each door, identifying the room where guests would stay. The engravings were names of flowers and coincidently could be used as women's names as well. Eight rooms, eight names--Violet, Rose, Daisy, and so forth--but the music she was hearing was coming from behind the door of the guest room with the nameplate that read Lily. Sarah was facing the door, transfixed by each letter, her own reflection staring back at her. After running her fingers over the etched surface, she reached for the doorknob in an effort to turn it, but it opened by itself. The music stopped.

The door led to a child's room, with painted wood floors, and a canopy bed neatly covered with a white eyelet quilt and blue satin ribbons strung through it. The way the toys were scattered around, it looked lived in, as if a child had still been playing, sleeping, and living in this room named Lily. Sarah thought for a moment and wondered if this room belonged to the same Lily from the letter she found under the porch. Could this be the same Lily that the mother's letter was addressed to? Could this room have belonged to Lily Rose? Sitting on the bed was an antique-looking dollhouse that looked similar to the Otter Cove. The dollhouse was opened, and inside, sitting next to the tiny doll furniture, was a music box. The lid was shut tight. Sarah reached in to pick it up and opened the lid, and the music started to play once again.

On the floor of the box was the skeleton key covered in dirt. The same key she found by the attic door. The same key that she held in her hands and that flew off under the porch. The same key she was not able to reach, and she was the only one that knew where it rested.

Woven in between the serrated notches was a blue satin ribbon.

Something was drawing her in, calling out to her—an unknown presence, an entity not to be questioned, but to confront, right here, right now.

Chapter 11

The Attic

Pieces of plaster came plummeting down from the ceiling, transporting Sarah immediately out of her trance. The resurrected key was back in her hands, and now an excruciating, intolerable, insufferable pounding, banging, slamming noise was coming from inside the walls. Although her mind said to flee, her feet were not cooperating, as if they were glued to the rickety hardwood planks beneath her. The old toys once sitting tranquil now turned to chaos, shaking and rattling, and they went sailing across the room one by one, immediately shattering to pieces on the cold wood floor. The pounding only strengthened with each passing moment, and this time it sent Sarah flying out of the room and straight up the staircase. Something was drawing her in, calling out to her--an unknown presence, an entity not to be questioned, but to confront, right here, right now.

The attic door that was once shut tight now was wide open, an invitation for Sarah to step inside as the only guest. The small attic space was dark and cold and smelled of mildew and mothballs, as was expected of such a place. As Sarah was fumbling around in the dreary darkness, a chain brushed up against her hair. Realizing what it was, she pulled on it twice. A soft light glowed over the room, and more evidence of what *used to be* conveyed itself. The amber-colored walls, the boxes and furniture draped with dingy linens, covered up and seemingly forgotten. Leaning against one of the four corners were large bolts of suede and plaid fabrics and an antique sewing machine with the thread and needle still in place.

Sarah let out a gasp after what she saw next sitting in the corner of the room. Her jaw dropped in total shock. A baffled Dickens was staring up at her, looking lost and scared out of his mind, not letting out even the slightest whimper. His blue leather collar was lying on the floor beside him and replaced by a piece of rope wrapped tightly around his neck. The makeshift leash reached over to the trunk sitting next to him and was tied to the rusty latch.

"Dickens, oh my God," Sarah said, running to his side. "Why didn't you bark, buddy?"

Sarah felt as if her body were floating above the room as she tried so desperately to come to terms with all that had been happening. Her salty tears rolling down her cheeks, she asked herself out loud, "Who could have done this to a defenseless animal? This has gone way beyond insane, or perhaps I am the one who is insane."

Sarah immediately untied Dickens, checking him out to make sure he was okay.

"You seem okay, buddy. You don't look hurt. I have been so worried about you."

Sarah stroked her hands through his short fur coat. Dickens panted heavily, elated he was back with his master. His eyes filled with an innocent uncertainty, but his focus soon turned to a more urgent matter. Something came over him, sending him in a whirlwind panic, making him scratch, sniff, and circle the old trunk that held him prisoner.

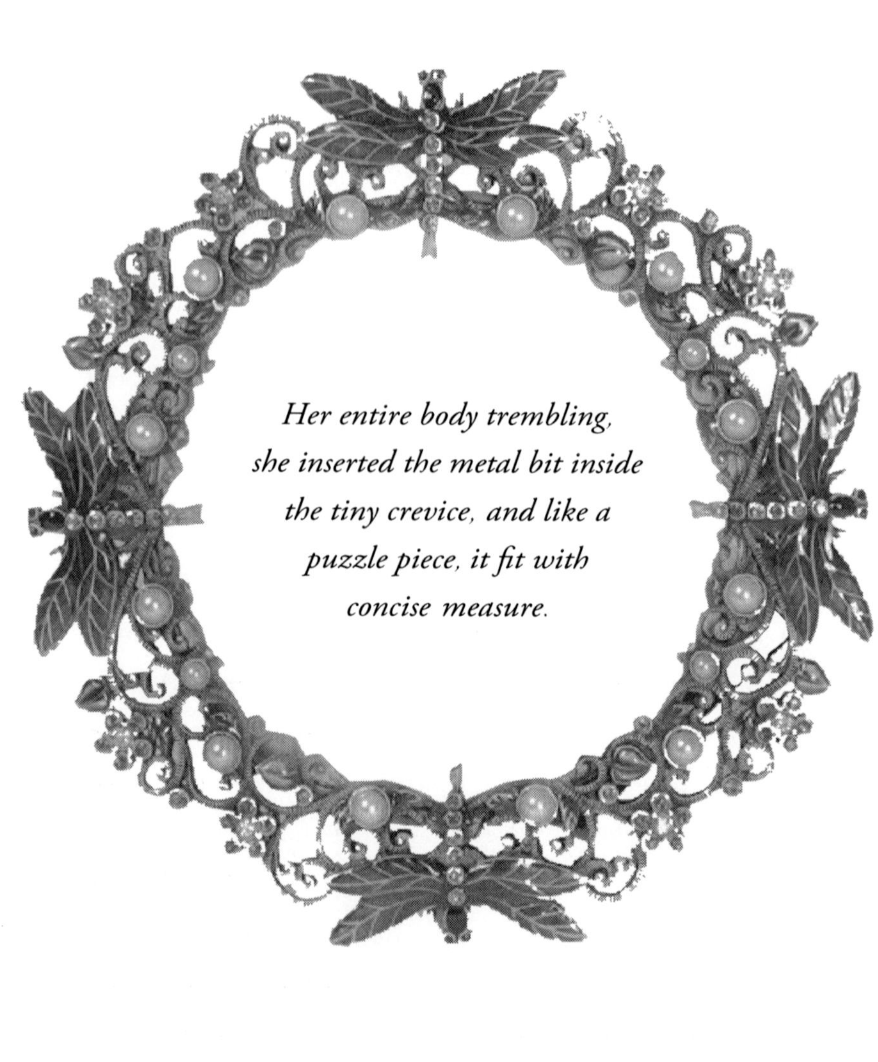

Her entire body trembling, she inserted the metal bit inside the tiny crevice, and like a puzzle piece, it fit with concise measure.

Chapter 12

With Concise Measure

The old abandoned steamer trunk was sealed tight with leather cowhide straps, a rusty latch, and a padlock. The paint, which was once solid green, was now chipped away by wear and tear and time, exposing the raw wood underneath. The brass-plated hardware was dented and worn, an apparent sign it had been put to good use at one time or another.

Inspecting the simple details, Sarah came to the realization that she literally held the key in her hands to this treasure trunk in more ways than one. Her entire body trembling, she inserted the metal bit inside the tiny crevice, and like a puzzle piece, it fit with concise measure.

She turned the barrel slightly, and first there was a clicking sound, and then a connection. The lock released, and Sarah's heart skipped a beat.

With Dickens close by, the lid lifted with ease, and now the contents that were once buried beneath the tarnished hinges were now exposed. Although it didn't appear to be a large trunk from the outside, the inside was spacious and surprisingly pleasant to the eye.

The sides of the trunk and drawers were covered with a delicate paper decorated with gold-leaf initials scattered about: AW, CW, AW, CW. Tucked in the drawers and nooks and crannies were bundled-up letters wrapped with twine, much like the one found under the porch, postcards, sewing patterns, and a jar of buttons, but what caught Sarah's eye almost immediately were the vast number of newspaper clippings. Shocking and true, the proverbial *Beacon Journal* she had discovered in town showed its ugly headlines once again. Each article had been torn from its master pages and with defined purpose neatly arranged in the trunk alongside the forgotten belongings. The articles each had large bold-faced lettering written by eager journalists to no avail putting in their two cents to solve an unsolvable mystery. All assumptions. Line by line, they were thinking that they had the answers. Was it murder? Was it suicide? Who or what killed these travelers that stayed in this old house on the hill?

The pounding noise abruptly returned even louder than before, making sure Sarah knew "it" was calling the shots. Taunting and teasing her by dragging her from one room to another like a rag doll, it was now taking its toll. Sarah scooped up the newspapers in one fell swoop. Stumbling and bumping into the furniture and boxes, she managed to make her way out of the attic in a hurry. No need to call out for Dickens, as he was not far behind. She grabbed the doorhandle and slammed the door shut, leaving behind the evil that seeped within the walls.

She hovered over the
antiquated archives, her eyes
drinking in each word,
searching for clues,
suspects from the past.

Chapter 13

The Only Witness

Sarah's eyelids felt heavy and were difficult to open at first, but sensing the light of day, she forced herself to open one lid at a time. Exhausted and disoriented, she assessed the room, and immediately the reality she had been living came flooding back. She was curled up on the sofa in the study, trying to comprehend how she managed to fall asleep in the first place. Her body was weak, but her mind was spiraling, confused, bewildered, yet determined.

Scattered on the floor next to the sofa were the newspapers that she found inside the old green trunk. Not wasting any time, she hovered over the antiquated archives, her eyes drinking in each word, searching for clues, suspects from the past.

As Sarah squinted to see the fine print, a recognizable name jumped off the page. She whispered it out loud to make it a reality. "Catherine and Andrew Willingsworth! Wait a minute … how do I know these people?"

Taking in a deep breath, she played it back in her head, envisioning inside the trunk, recalling the gold initials, the painting in the hallway, the letter she found under the porch. She was surrounded by this couple, their belongings, their lives, their family pictures. This had to be their house. It had always belonged to them. She sensed it; she felt it.

Sarah couldn't read the article fast enough, jumping around, stumbling, tongue-tied, rushing her way through to find out more details.

Holding the paper up close to her face, she read the captions and bylines first. A habit she had developed a long time ago as a journalist, to come up with the titles for her articles, was one of her favorite pastimes and a way to suck in the reader. This article's headline: "Was It an Accident, or Was It Murder?" by C. H. Henesy, published September 12, 1952.

She read it out loud:

"Innkeepers Catherine and Andrew Willingsworth were found dead on the second floor of Otter Cove. No murder weapon; no sign of forced entry. Their eight-year-old

daughter, known to be the only witness, ran from the scene, fell to her death. Although assumed dead, her body was never to be found. The crime happened almost 200 years ago."

"Oh my God! Jacob Walker was telling the truth."

Jacob Walker--the ghostly stranger that came to the inn without warning to give his warning, a man that had been dead for all these years. But why would C. H. Henesy want to bring this story back to life? Why was it so important to this journalist to set the record straight?

The phone rang three or four times before Sarah even realized it, but this time it wasn't her cell phone. For the first time since Sarah arrived at the inn, a phone that she didn't even know existed was ringing, calling out to her, screaming for attention. The black rotary-dial phone was hidden behind a lamp and a stack of books on the end table next to the sofa.

Apprehensive, but curious, she picked up the receiver and in a soft-spoken voice said … "Hello."

The connection wasn't too good, as there was static on the other end, but Sarah could sense there was someone there. She tried again to get the person on the other end to say something, anything.

"Hello, is anyone there?"

"Where is my mommy?"

It was a child's voice. The little girl sounded distant, and her words were barely audible, making them difficult to understand.

"Did you say, where is your mommy? I think you have the wrong number." Sarah waited for a response.

More static came through the line, and her words were garbled, but the little girl asked again, "Where is my mommy?"

Before Sarah could respond, the line went dead--no dial tone, no static. The voice on the other end was now silent. Sarah set the receiver back on the cradle and then followed the cord in an attempt to see where it led, where it was plugged in. It wasn't. She took a step backward, her clammy hands raised to her mouth, unsure if she should let out a frightened scream. She backed out of the study, never taking her eyes off the cradled receiver. The phone rang.

Sarah fell straight to her knees,
the phone now in her grasp,
but her heart and conscience
were in conflict.

Chapter 14

Through Her Tears

Stumbling down the long, narrow corridor, the phone in the study still ringing, buzzing, humming in her ears, Sarah had one objective in mind, and that was to get out of the room and call someone, anyone. Beyond hysterical, she was pushing, pulling herself along the walls and furniture, using whatever leverage needed to reach the foyer as fast as possible.

Through her tears, she grabbed her satchel from the hall tree and turned it upside down, shaking it and frantically searching for her cell phone. As the contents of her life spilled out and landed hard on the floor, she caught a glimpse of her silver Nokia spinning out of control until finally stalling by her feet. Sarah fell straight to her knees, the phone now in her grasp, but her heart and conscience were in conflict. The logical choice was to call the authorities, but for some reason, her fingers went in another direction. Sarah gripped the phone, willing her little sister to pick up.

It rang a couple of times, and a familiar voice was on the other end.

"Hello, this is Abigail."

"Abby, I'm so glad you are home. Listen, I'm staying at a bed-and-breakfast in Cape Elizabeth, Maine, working on my book. Did Mom and Dad tell you?"

"Wait … who is this?"

"Jesus, Abby, it's me! Can you come here? I don't think I've been so scared in my life."

Sarah stood up and nervously paced back and forth, waiting for her response…. There was a long, awkward silence.

"Abs, you there?"

"This isn't funny," Abby responded with a harsh tone. "I'm hanging up."

"Hold on a minute. It's me, Sarah!"

"Sarah's dead," Abby snapped. Her sobbing could be heard muffled through the phone.

"Whoever this is, I hope you know it is cruel what you

are doing. You can go to hell."

She hung up.

Sarah threw her phone across the room, and immediately sank to the floor, crying, sobbing, and now questioning even her own mortality. Dickens leaned against her at first, but then lay down next to her, pressing his wet nose against her knee.

"No, Dickens, we can't let it beat us; let's get out of here."

Sarah stood up and scrambled to find her shoes. She slipped them on and then headed out the front door and ran straight for the jagged rocks.

The ocean waters were turbulent, showing no mercy whatsoever to anyone or anything. The fog was rolling in, riding the waves toward the craggy shoreline. Sarah, turning around to face the house in turmoil, was relieved to be on the outside looking in. With great intensity, her eyes traveled from the porch to the roof, stopping hard at the attic window. She caught a glimpse of a dark shadow standing at the window, looking down, watching her every move through the tinted glass.

The perimeter of the lighthouse was surrounded by a wrought-iron fence inundated with thorny vines slithering between each weathered stake.

Chapter 15

The Eyes of the Sea

The gravel pathway leading to the lighthouse was a short distance from the rocks, and for the first time, Sarah found herself standing just a few feet away. She was out of breath from running down the path. The perspective this close up was so different from behind the windowpane in the study. From the study, it was surreal and untouchable, but now that it was right in front of her face, it seemed ordinary and familiar.

The perimeter was surrounded by a wrought-iron fence inundated with thorny vines slithering between each weathered stake. Besides an old wicker chair and a broken handcart lying on its side in the yard, the property appeared to be vacant.

Sarah was not quite sure why she was standing at the lighthouse door, but was surprising even herself. Her fist started knocking. A stern, but muffled, voice penetrated the pores of the splintered wood, rumbling in Sarah's ear … "Whatever you are selling, I am not buying,"

"I promise you, I am not selling anything; I just have a few questions. Do you have a few minutes?" Sarah said, looking over her shoulder, still feeling as if someone was watching. She tried to shake it off.

His throat was scratchy and coarse.

"I have nothing to say to you or anyone. Now get the hell off my property."

"Your property--are you sure? Because I was under the impression you were the lighthouse keeper and did not own this place."

"This is a small town, miss. People say things. You can think what you want, as I honestly don't care what people say about me."

"You know, I don't have time for games, sir. I just need to know if you have firsthand information about the couple that were killed inside The Otter Cove Inn, the same inn where I am staying. Is it true that they were murdered? They are simple questions--either you do or don't."

Sarah, gripping onto the doorframe, leaned into it in an attempt to hear a reaction from the faceless stranger. Not a sound was coming from the lighthouse keeper; the only sound was the quiet surf crashing up against the rocks.

Sarah, now growing impatient, said, "This is ridiculous. Could you please have the decency to open the door and at least look me in the eye?"

It wasn't too long after her comment that the voice coming from behind the door made an attempt to communicate face to face. The clicking, twists, and turns of what seemed like several locks and latches at last concluded with the door opening just a couple of inches. It was obvious he was guarded; the only things visible at this point were his bloodshot eyes and deep wrinkles, magnified behind his thick dark-rimmed glasses. His haunting and unsympathetic stare was not a welcome that Sarah anticipated.

"What do you want?"

"I was hoping we could talk about the inn."

"Go on."

"My stay at the inn has been interesting, to say the least, and the things that have been happening to me and my dog have been on the lines of supernatural. What can you tell me about it? Do you know anything about the murders that took place, the ghostly happenings? Or maybe I am just crazy. Wait … don't answer that one."

Sarah turned her head just for a second to check on Dickens' whereabouts and to bide the old man some time to gather his words. With the fog now on shore, the visibility was getting worse, and she could barely make out the silhouette of Dickens sniffing in the yard.

"I know you are staying at the inn. I have seen you puttering around on the grounds." Pushing back his glasses with his feeble, crooked fingers, he studied Sarah's eyes, as if he wanted her to read his thoughts.

"Okay, I wouldn't exactly call it puttering around, but if that is the way you would like to put it, I will go with that. And you have been watching me, really? I find that just a little disturbing," Sarah said, annoyed with his rude and blunt delivery.

Still peering through the small crack of the door, he went on.

"Look, I haven't been watching you. My job is to watch the sea, and yes, I can tell you some stories about the inn, but I had nothing to do with the murders of …."

He stopped himself abruptly.

"I wasn't accusing, just asking, and you didn't finish your sentence. Why is that?"

He looked away.

"Can I please come inside?" Sarah pleaded.

He opened the door reluctantly and nodded his approval for her to step inside the tight quarters.

"You know, I am more than just a lighthouse keeper. I am the eyes of the sea, the one that guides the lost fishermen in these rough waters and brings them safely to shore. They depend on me and the beacon of this lighthouse. Do I make myself clear?"

"Crystal," Sarah said, holding up the palms of her hands in front of her, surrendering to her supposed ignorance.

It was dark and cramped inside and smelled like stale beer and cheap whiskey. There was natural light coming in from an oval window that was deeply recessed in the painted brick walls. A dingy recliner and side table took up most of the room, and scattered all over the place were wooden ships intricately carved down to the finest point of the sails. The most extravagant feature in the room was a circular staircase. A thin piece of rope was used as the makeshift handrail that would guide those that would climb the staircase's narrow steps to reach the tower.

Now that they were face to face, Sarah took a moment to analyze the situation. She was surprised by her bravery to step inside a stranger's home alone, which goes way beyond anything and everything her mother taught her growing up. In fact, now that the door was closed behind her, all that she had learned went straight down the toilet.

"My mother would kill me if she knew where I was right now," she whispered under her breath.

"What did you say? You're going to have to speak up, miss; I can't hear a damn thing."

He stood about five feet tall, hunched over from age. His stained trousers and disheveled appearance paralleled his character to a tee. His thick black glasses were rigged together by a gold safety pin. It was endearing and sad at the same time. Adjusting them slightly, aware of her observation, he broke the uncomfortable silence.

"They belonged to my late wife, and I like wearing them; they give me comfort."

"By all means; I wasn't judging."

"Well, you got your way; you managed to push yourself inside my home, didn't you?"

Sarah didn't know what to say to his comment.

"What, now you are speechless? Well, whatever you have to say, make it quick; I have work to do."

As Sarah scrambled for hurried words, her eyes wandered the perimeter walls and stopped sharp on an award plaque inscribed to a Charles Howard Henesy for Excellence in Investigative Reporting.

The shock of disbelief was written all over Sarah's face, and now it was apparent to the lighthouse keeper, a.k.a. the Eyes of the Sea, that she had put some of the pieces together and figured him out.

Sarah was fumbling to form her mouth to fit her words she was desperately seeking.

"It was you .... You wrote the article about the murders in the inn, the presence wandering the hallways; it was your byline. You were ... I mean, you are C. H. Henesy."

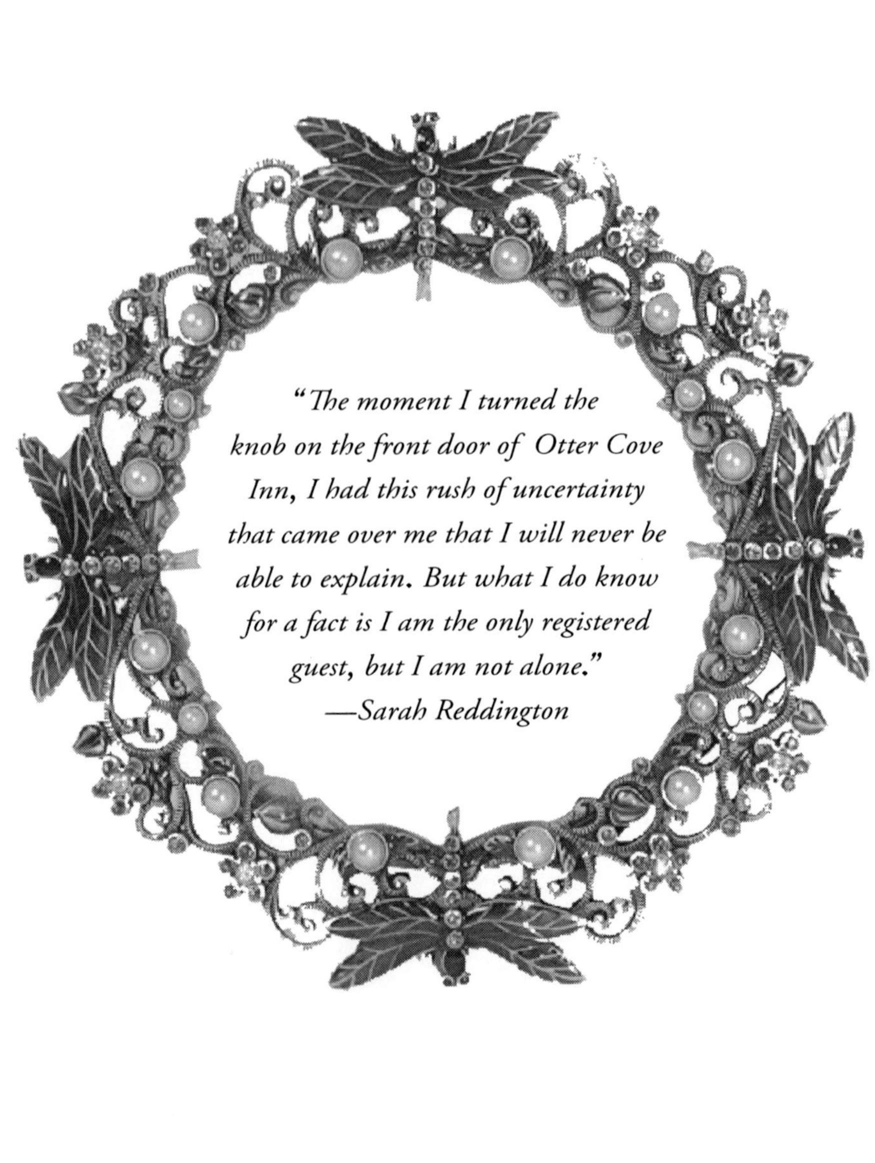
"The moment I turned the
knob on the front door of Otter Cove
Inn, I had this rush of uncertainty
that came over me that I will never be
able to explain. But what I do know
for a fact is I am the only registered
guest, but I am not alone."
—Sarah Reddington

Chapter 16

A Rigid Conversation

His resentment opened an old wound, exposing the underlying emotional distress all over again. The bitterness that Charles H. Henesy was holding on to was oozing from his pores. His stance was rigid, and the scowl on his face would shock anyone at first glance.

"I can see by your demeanor that this conversation is not going to be easy for you. I'll try to make it quick," Sarah said, wishing she had pen and paper in hand.

He glanced down at his tattered shoes and then back up again. This time his eyes met hers directly.

"What did you say your name was, miss?" he said, clenching his narrow jaw.

"Sarah."

"I don't like having conversations with anyone, especially pushy strangers."

Sarah could feel her body shaking inside and was hopeful it wasn't noticeable on the outside.

"But you are a journalist; the proof of that is on the wall."

"Not anymore."

"Why hide behind this façade?"

"Facade, hardly; this is who I am now. What do you think, I just cower inside this old lighthouse and drown my sorrows in hard liquor? You are wrongly mistaken. I suggest you make your point."

Sarah readied herself to explain her situation. In spite of everything, she was determined to tell her story in order to get to the bottom of the chaos that surrounded her.

"I promise you that it was not my intention to travel to Maine to be haunted by ghosts or to seek you out and harass you, Mr. Henesy. I am not sure about a lot of things on so many levels since I arrived in Cape Elizabeth. The moment I turned the knob on the front door of Otter Cove Inn, I had this rush of uncertainty that came over me that I will never be able to explain. But what I do know for a fact is I am the only registered guest, but I am not alone."

"What do you mean by that?" His body shifted with nervous curiosity.

"Do you mind if I sit for a minute?" Sarah asked, feeling lightheaded.

"I guess." He motioned to the only chair in the room.

Sarah made her way over to it and sat on the edge, the cushion soiled and worn. She waited a few minutes before she explained.

"I have been hearing noises and witnessing unexplained incidents inside the house. There is a constant pounding in the walls, which is making me think that I am losing my mind. My challenge now is to try to decipher between what is imagination and what is crazy. I stumbled upon a stack of old newspaper articles dated back in the mid-1900s. There was one noteworthy story that captured my attention, and now, for an added twist, the writer is standing right in front of me. I am sure you can understand the reasons why I came knocking on your door, as I needed to talk to someone; it was meant to be you. My stay at the inn was supposed to be a getaway to write my novel and surround myself in research, but the paranormal distractions have led me down another path, and the path was directly to you, Mr. Henesy."

His expression was puzzling, as he took off his glasses and rubbed his tired eyes.

"Whatever I wrote in that article, or any article, for that matter, was never taken seriously." He put his glasses back on his face.

"How do you explain the award plaque on the wall with your name on it?"

"That was before The Otter Cove Inn nightmare, before it turned into a media fiasco," he said with a smirk.

"Fiasco, how so?"

"I was laughed right out of the newspaper building. Not one damn person believed my story, not one. I was just a kid, anyway, a rookie; nobody listens to kids." He rolled his eyes with annoyance.

"You would have thought that the editor of the paper would have been supportive, backed you up on your story," Sarah said, trying to get on his good side.

"You would have thought that, now, wouldn't you? But I was a stubborn fool and kept pushing my luck like I always do, asking for more ink, more real estate, preferably front-page. But the more I wrote, the more they cut, slashed and eventually tossed. I wanted the truth to come out somehow, and through my printed words was, in my opinion, the perfect plan. I was tired of everyone thinking that what happened inside The Otter Cove Inn was a legend or a myth. That's why I brought the story back from the grave." He picked up one of his wooden boats and examined it, seemingly stalling the moment.

"Did you disclose your story to the police?"

"Police? What a joke. You're damn right I went to the police. They patrolled the inn for days, searched inside, even spent the night, but didn't find anything on the premises to match my story. The presence did not care to entertain such distinguished guests that night, and after the police gave their report, they were quoted in the newspaper, 'It' came not. That is when things got ugly. They called me crazy, which spread to the locals. They, in turn, thought that since I was a writer, my imagination and ability to write fiction got the best of me and I lied, made it all up to sell papers. I was humiliated right out of a job, and I haven't written a word since. When I look back now, I wish I would have never set one foot inside that old place."

He walked over to the small window and stared up at the inn, his hands resting on the edge of his pants pockets.

"How did you manage to get your story?"

"I needed to earn extra money, so I knocked on the door and was hired on the spot to do odd jobs. I suppose you could say I was a jack-of-all-trades. I had no idea this would get me so much copy for the paper. The story became my obsession."

The color drained from Mr. Henesy's cheeks, and his breathing became rapid. His cold, gray eyes filled with anger, resentment, and now what appeared to be tainted memories from all those years ago.

"What ever happened inside that house, Mr. Henesy? You can tell me. I am staying at the inn, and I am living it. I need to know that I am not crazy, please."

"I tried over and over again to tell someone, anyone who would listen, but they ignored me. I worked every day for an entire summer. The inn was always filled with guests, and there was so much to do at all times. On one occasion, I can remember standing on the staircase a few steps from the third floor, busy painting or fixing something, and the pounding noise would make its grand entrance. It was unbearable, but it seemed I was the only one that could hear it. I saw two dead bodies lying on the floor near the attic door, and I called out a desperate plea for help. Random guests came flying out of their rooms, curious, of course; even the innkeepers would come running to my rescue, but once they reached the top of the stairs, the bodies were no longer there. They disappeared as fast as they appeared. There was nothing normal about that house, and I cannot even believe it is still standing. It should have been condemned a long time ago, torn down and burned." He looked away in disgust.

"Go on, Mr. Henesy; I'm listening."

"If you are 'living it,' why do you want to know my story?"

"I just need to know that I am not crazy." Sarah adjusted herself in the seat.

"Very well, I will tell you some of the things that happened to me, but I have tried for years to erase this recurring nightmare from my memory."

He sat down on the edge of the side table and paused for just a couple of minutes.

Sarah interjected, "Forgive me, but was it a nightmare for you, or was it a reality?"

"Perhaps after hearing what I am about to say, you can judge for yourself based on your own experiences. So, do you mind if I continue?"

"Yes, please. I'm sorry; please, of course, go on. "

Mr. Henesy cleared his throat and painfully dug up his past.

"There were days when nothing would happen at all, and then some days were filled with all sorts of strange things. Oddly enough, the furniture would move by itself, the temperature would change from one extreme to another. The guest room doors would open and shut and sometimes lock by themselves. I could swear one time while I was walking through the kitchen, someone tapped me on the shoulder, but when I turned around, there was nobody there."

The old man inhaled the stagnant air, his hands trembling.

"Where did you find these newspaper articles?"

"In the attic."

"You went in the attic?"

"Yes," Sarah said, now feeling uneasy, as his tone switched gears.

"What made you do such a stupid thing as to go behind those doors?" Did you take anything out of that room, other than the old newspapers, anything at all? The old man's arms were doing most of the talking.

"No, I don't think so, just the newspaper articles and the key to the …."

He interrupted her before she could finish.

"You have to put them back. 'It' won't like it that you took those things, as it knows when things go missing."

"You are scaring me. What is this 'it' you are talking about?"

"'It' is the entity that controls the inn from within the walls. The spirit that makes damn sure every soul that enters the wooden-frame structure has no choice but to question his or her own sanity. The 'it' I am referring to is known as 'the innkeeper.' No one can see it, no one can touch it, but they can sense its presence. The Keeper's ultimate goal is to drive whoever is in its presence completely insane, insane enough to commit murder and insane enough to commit suicide. When this is achieved, it wins. It keeps the house. It takes care of the house until the next sane person walks through the door, and then … the games begin."

This horrific story brought Sarah to her feet and backing out toward the entryway, her immediate escape. It was time to go; she was no longer welcome. She opened the door and stepped outside, turning around to face him, now confused and terrified. He grabbed onto the doorknob with extreme force and spoke the final words of their rigid conversation: "Get out of that house before it's too late."

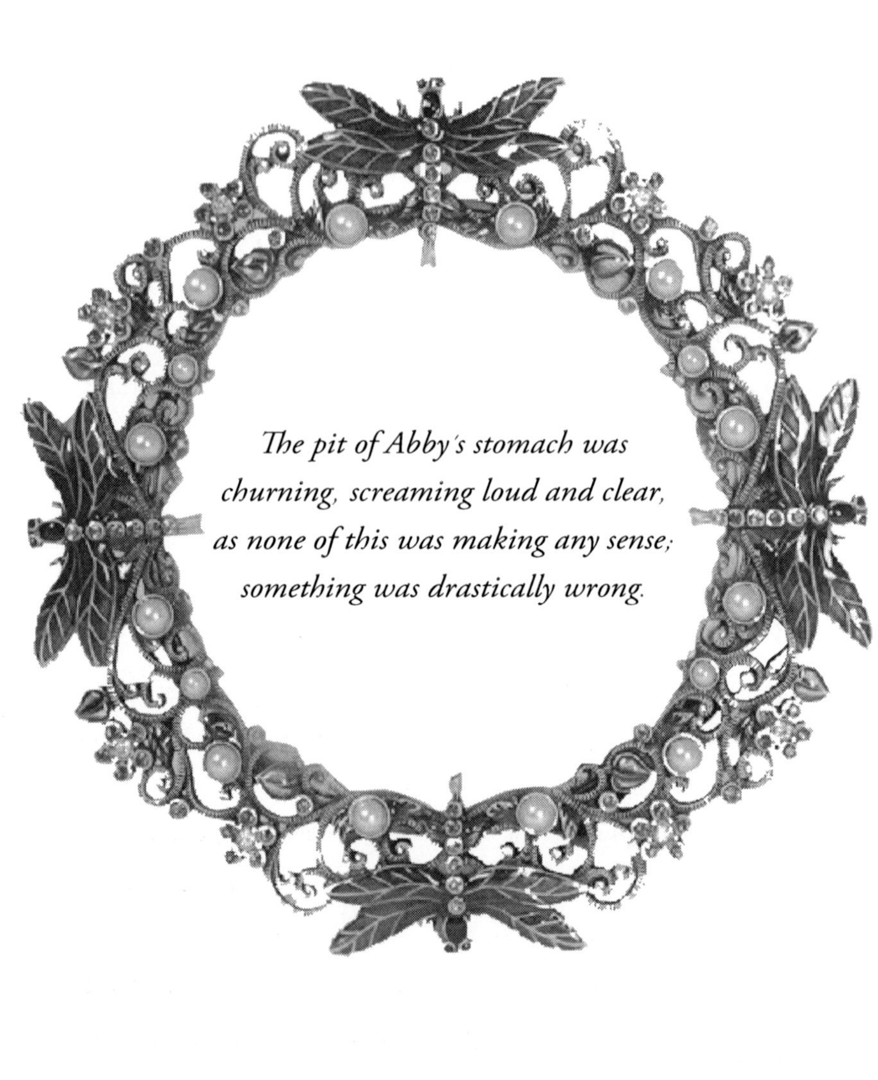

The pit of Abby's stomach was churning, screaming loud and clear, as none of this was making any sense; something was drastically wrong.

Chapter 17

Sisters to the Core

The fog was suspended inches above the ground, giving that eerie abandoned look on the streets of Portland. The windshield wipers on Abigail's blue Ranger were working overtime in an effort to keep up with the mist ricocheting off of the winding concrete. Just below the truck tires' edge was the steep and treacherous Atlantic Ocean shore.

Tessa, Abby's six-year-old daughter, was sleeping sound in the backseat, clutching her well-loved teddy. She had been withdrawn for months since her parents' separation, and now having to take this unexpected trip to Portland only added to the long list of emotional complications.

Abby glanced back in the rearview mirror at her slumbering daughter, wishing things could have been different somehow, that she could have given her a happily-ever-after ending, but that was not the case. Her marriage was far from a fairy tale, and at this stage of the game, it seemed hopeless.

Abby depended on her big sister for so many things, but getting Abby through the toughest times while her marriage was crumbling was a true godsend. Sarah had been both unassuming and a good listener, which allowed her to be a realist without all of the added bullshit. Only nineteen months apart, sisters to the core, Abby and Sarah looked nothing alike, but the similarities they did share came from the heart. Their conversations at family gatherings were somewhat comical, as Abby and Sarah would finish each other's sentences on a whim, annoying for some, but amusing to each other.

At this point, Abby was thinking the worst, not hearing a word from her sister for almost three weeks now--no e-mails, not even a text message. When Abby tried to call Sarah's cell phone, it just went directly to voice mail, which was full. Sarah's publisher hadn't heard from her since the first day she arrived in Maine, their conversation brief and all business. Sarah was sensitive to her publisher's needs, and to not contact her for all this time was beyond disturbing. After all, Sarah had a deadline to meet. Of course, her publisher was oblivious, and most likely it wouldn't have crossed her mind if it wasn't for Abby's calling her office and asking her straight out.

The pit of Abby's stomach was churning, screaming loud and clear, as none of this was making any sense; something was drastically wrong.

Tears rolled down her pale, freckled cheeks, and Abby lightly swept them away, careful to avoid encountering the *WHY* questions from Tessa. She just wasn't prepared to explain to her daughter that her aunt was missing; she needed more time.

A good mother as always, Abby wanted to protect her baby girl and keep things light and breezy as to not lead to the real reason why they were traveling to Maine.

Abby was feeling somewhat relieved she had a substitute teacher to cover her art class while she was away. Although teaching was her passion, art was her life. It was her hope to someday have an art studio, sell thousands of dollars worth of paintings, and become a household name. It would be a dream come true to see an Abigail Grey piece hanging on every wall in the New England region.

Straining her tear-filled eyes, she could barely see the highway, let alone the signs through the thick fog, and using her high beams somehow made it worse. In the distance, she could see a road sign coming up, positive it was the exit they needed to their final destination.

"Tessa, wake up, sweetie girl. Mommy needs your help."

"What is it, Mommy? Where are we?" Tessa said, rubbing her sleepy eyes.

"I do believe we are on State Road 22, or at least we are supposed to be. With all this fog, I can't be so sure, my love."

"Are we almost to our hotel? How many more minutes, Mommy?"

"Well, I'm not sure, but according to this trusty map I just realized I was holding upside down, maybe five or ten minutes. Can you stand it, my love? Now help Mommy find the big hotel, okay?"

"K." Tessa adjusted herself in her seat so she could see out the window better.

"What color is the hotel, Mommy?"

"The brochure shows the picture; here, you look at it." Abby handed the brochure over her shoulder, which was awkward, but did the job. Tessa reached up to grab it from her mommy's reach, all the while still talking in her sweet six-year-old voice--the tiny voice all parents want to hold on to forever.

"I am thinking there will be lots of people at the hotel. Is that what you are thinking, Mommy?" Tessa said, studying the brochure from top to bottom, her feet bouncing up and down on the car seat.

Abby's eyes met her daughter's in the rearview mirror. "Maybe. I am not sure."

"I am thinking that everybody knows everybody. Are you thinking that too, Mommy?"

"Yep, Tessa, I'm thinking! But right now I am thinking we should be looking much harder, my love."

"Fine. I will try."

"Thank you, Tessa girl. I knew I could count on my little navigator. The good news is the next exit will take us to our hotel, or as they call it in Maine, inn. The Inn at St. John's is where we are going, smack in the middle of downtown Portland on a street called Congress. I heard that it is close to the museum--isn't that great news?"

"I guess, Mommy, but I still don't know why we have to come to this place."

"Hey, kiddo, it's going to be okay; we are going to be fine. This is a grown-up thing Mommy needs to take care of, that's all." Abigail turned around quickly to get a good look at her daughter's face. The sadness in her six-year-old eyes was heartbreaking to witness.

"Did you hear my words, Tessa girl?"

"I miss Daddy."

"I know you do, Tess. I know."

They turned onto Congress Street, and immediately

Abby had this overwhelming feeling that they were dropping out of time and place. It was night and day from the damp and misty highway they had just traveled on for the past three hours. The street was narrow, with huge shady trees draping their branches over the uneven brick pavers. The speed limit was set at twenty-five miles per hour, giving those that traveled through it the have-no-choice scenic view straight from the comfort of their cars. The row of Victorian houses, shops, and a turn-of-the-century fire station was tastefully appointed with rich style and character.

After traveling just a few minutes down this quaint and charming street, they came to a four-way stop, perhaps the only one for miles. Straight ahead was a black-and-white wooden sign, giving its clear and concise directions to get to The Inn at St. John's. She needed to turn left here.

Abby pulled into the parking lot and found a convenient spot near the front door, put the truck in park, and turned off the engine. After pushing the release button on her seat belt, she gathered her belongings, opened the truck door, and stepped out on solid ground. It felt good to be here, knowing she was one step closer to finding her sister.

Abby opened up the back door and unbuckled her daughter's seat belt, giving her a quick peck on her forehead.

"Here we go, Tessa. Let's go check out the inside of

this place, what do you say?"

"It looks old," Tessa whined. "Do you think it has a pool?" Tessa said, glaring up at the four-story dwelling, all the while swinging her bear by his tattered arms.

"It does look old, but most of these places are old, and old is not always a bad thing, cutie girl. Now stop your complaining, and hold on to my hand, please."

They entered the double doors and went into the lobby, and in the dead center of the room was a remarkable crystal chandelier illuminating the polished dark wood floors and warm, textured walls. There was a pianist in the far corner playing a quiet melody while a young couple stood close by, taking in the free entertainment. The fragrance in the room was a mix of fresh-cut flowers, baked goods, and assorted teas.

Behind the desk was a gentleman in his mid-forties, with thinning dark brown hair and wire-rimmed glasses. He looked up from his busy work to acknowledge Abby and Tessa by giving a nod and a smile. In a confident, proud voice, he said, "Welcome to The Inn at St. John's. My name is Robert Cooper. I am the owner. How may I help you?"

"Hello. Thank you, Mr. Cooper. It is good to finally be here. My name is Abigail Grey, and this is my daughter, Tessa."

"Please call me Bob."

"Okay, Bob. I hope you can help me. I do have a reservation, but first I wanted to ask you a question."

Abby turned around to make sure Tessa hadn't wandered too far from her sight. She could see that she was busy twirling and dancing with her bear to the music.

"Do you have a guest registered here by the name of Sarah Reddington? She was supposed to have checked in quite some time ago. I'm her sister."

After tugging once on his burgundy vest, he pulled out a black leather journal from underneath the counter, opened it up, and then smoothed out the lined paper.

"Sarah Reddington … her name sounds familiar, but I am not picturing her face."

Sliding his finger down the crème pages, skimming the names of past guests from several weeks ago, who are now by far a distant memory, he quietly whispered Sarah's name under his breath. He turned page after page, and his finger paused, tapping lightly on her name in bold black ink with the date of her supposed arrival.

The gentleman folded his hands together and looked up from the journal and right into Abby's eyes.

"You are correct, my dear; she did indeed have a reservation, but she never checked in."

The only light on in the entire house was coming from the third floor, flickering like an unsteady, wavering candle in the breeze.

Chapter 18

Without Warning

The bellman guided Abby and Tessa up the impressive staircase just off the main gathering room. The red, black, and gold speckled carpet draped elegantly over each step, exposing the rich cherry wood on the ends. The floral wallpaper was poised with timeless art, tapestries, and candle sconces. The young man carried their two small suitcases with ease, tucking one under his arm and holding on to the other in his right hand. He introduced himself as a student of American history and was working at The Inn at St. John's part time to help out his parents with the dreaded college tuition. He didn't mention his name, but his nametag read "Patrick." On the way to the fourth, and top, floor, he gave what sounded like a well-rehearsed spiel, sharing a few key points on the history of the inn, what time period the furnishings were made, and which distant, deceased relative was posing in the oil paintings. He spoke his words with articulate grace, steady, yet deliberate, editing and correcting himself throughout his dissertation with the appropriate facts and dates applied.

"Just so you folks know, this inn was built in 1867, and it is listed on the National Register of Historic Places. It took eighteen months of renovation and a ton of cash to get this old house in the impeccable shape it is in today. If it wasn't for the Coopers pouring their heart and soul into this project, it would have been condemned and demolished a long time ago. I know that might not be important to you, but it happens to be my major, the history part, I mean."

"Well, thank you for the history lesson; we have been paying attention, I promise," Abby said, squeezing Tessa's hand, sort of half telling the truth to young Patrick.

"These paintings are incredible. I love oil paintings. I teach high school art back home," Abby said proudly.

"Wow, that's awesome. Where's home?"

"Massachusetts, but I am originally from Chicago. We

moved to Mass about three years ago, against my better judgment."

"What do you like to paint?"

"Whatever inspires me, but mostly architecture, old buildings, doors, windows. I am constantly sketching something and never leave home without a sketchpad in tow."

They arrived at their bedchambers, room 4B. Patrick keyed the door and flipped on the light switch with his elbow, and then he presented the room with enthusiastic appreciation.

"So, are you here on business or pleasure?" It was Patrick's way of making small talk.

"Actually, we are here on a family issue; it's personal."

"Oh, so sorry to have been nosey. We just like to get to know our guests--makes them feel at home."

"No problem. I appreciate your asking."

There was a slight awkward moment of silence, but they moved through it, and Patrick went on with his presentation.

"Okay, here is your key. Please let us know if you need anything. Just press the number 3 on the phone, and we will be at your service. That goes for you too, young lady," and he whispered, "Ice cream with sprinkles" in Tessa's ear. Tessa's eyes widened with joy.

Abby thanked the young man and slipped him a few dollars for his assistance and guided tour, and then she shut the door and locked it.

The room was cozy and just enough space for two people to move around without bumping into each other. The twin beds were pushed up against the slanted pale blue walls, each bed layered with handmade quilts and lacey throw pillows. The painted writing desk in the corner was softened with a vase of flowers, vintage picture frames, and a black push-button phone. Tucked next to the phone was a trifold menu of what was available from the kitchen, apparently open twenty-four hours, self-serve after 9 o'clock, according to the fine print.

"Tessa, you need to get ready for bed," Abby said with an exhausted tone in her voice.

"But why? I'm hungry," Tessa pleaded.

"I know you are. Mommy will order us something, but first put your pajamas on." Abby's patience was running on empty.

Tessa reluctantly pulled out her suitcase and opened it up in search of her favorite pj's.

Abby ordered them a sandwich to share and some cold drinks. While waiting for the tap on the door, she paced the floor, feeling more anxious now than ever. She was convinced it was going to be a long and sleepless night.

Abby was sitting on the edge of the bed in total darkness, her thoughts spinning, spiraling out of control, and even though her daughter was in the bed next to her, she never felt more alone. Her eyes were wide open, and the conversation with the innkeeper kept rewinding and playing back in her head over and over again. He skimmed the guests' names page after page, line after line, as if he was looking for something in the lost and found box, an object, a set of keys. She so wanted him to make her feel better, to make things right again, to say the words she so wanted to hear.

Abby could feel her body starting to give out, her eyes struggling to stay open; she was willing to surrender and let the sleep wash over her.

The only light on in the entire house was coming from the third floor, flickering like an unsteady, wavering candle in the breeze. The front door was wide open, slamming violently up against the blue clapboard siding, shattering the glass panes into tiny slivers, sending the sharp pieces crashing onto the wooden planks of the wraparound porch. Sitting alone on the swing was a porcelain doll wearing a white eyelet dress and black shoes, with blue satin ribbons tied in her wavy blonde hair. The doll's chocolate brown eyes were cold and still staring straight ahead as the swing rocked itself back and forth and back and forth. The only sound the swing was making was coming from the metal hooks grating against the corroded chains.

She stood in the doorway, her body quivering and her bare feet bloody from walking through the broken glass. Without warning, the screaming began. The shrill screams echoed from the top of the stairs straight into her soul as she witnessed the twisted body tumbling down, helpless, crumbling, breaking, and rolling over each step until it reached the bottom … lifeless, limp, and quiet.

Falling to her knees, horrified by the thought of who or what could do such a thing, she prepared herself for what she was about to see. Exhaling her warm breath, now visible as it mixed with the cold, damp air, she turned the body over onto its back. Her eyes locked onto the face of this dead person, and she screamed …. It can't be; it's not possible. Oh my God, Sarah …

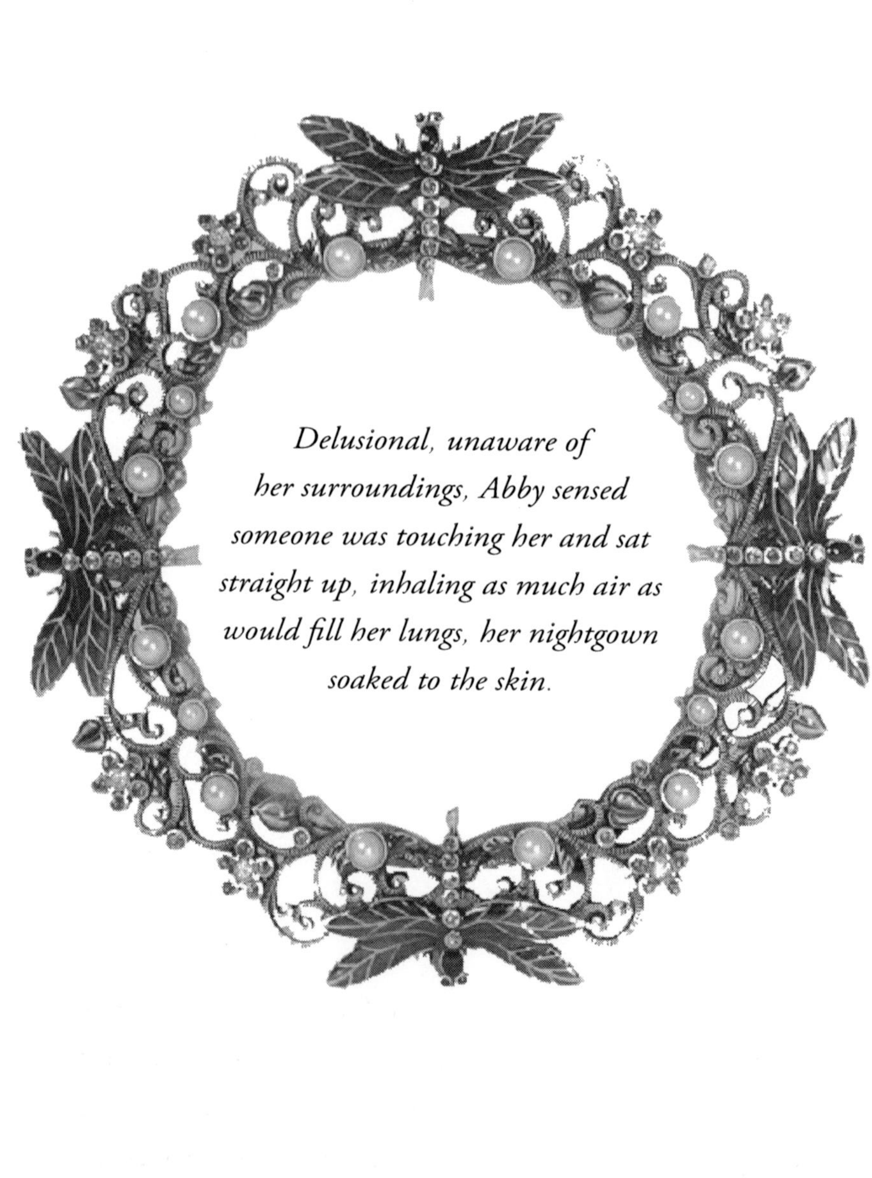

Delusional, unaware of her surroundings, Abby sensed someone was touching her and sat straight up, inhaling as much air as would fill her lungs, her nightgown soaked to the skin.

Chapter 19

Reflection in the Mirror

"Mommy, wake up! Please wake up!"

Tessa was standing next to her mommy's bed, shaking her with all her strength. Abby was in a deep sleep and having a horrific nightmare. The tears streaming down Tessa's cheeks, she was so frightened that her mommy was sick or in pain.

"Sarah, no, please, not Sarah," she pleaded, her head shifting from side to side on the pillow. Delusional, unaware of her surroundings, Abby sensed someone was touching her and sat straight up, inhaling as much air as would fill her lungs, her nightgown soaked to the skin.

With panic in Abby's voice, she screamed out, "Sarah, is that you?"

"No, Mommy; it's me, Tessa," she said through her tears.

Abby, starting to come to her senses, recognized her daughter was out of bed, and by the look on her face could see that she was scared to death.

"Tessa, oh my God, sweetie; I am so sorry to have scared you. It's okay; I'm okay. I was dreaming, that's all." Tessa climbed up into her mommy's arms, and Abby held on tight to her innocent little girl. They quietly rocked and soothed each other until they both calmed down and fell back asleep.

Morning came in a hurry, and Tessa was still snuggled up next to her mommy. Abby's eyes barely open and adjusting to the daylight that was peering in from between the curtains, she slipped out from under the covers and tiptoed straight into the bathroom. She stared at her reflection in the mirror, distraught at what she saw, as it looked as if someone had beaten her up and thrown her from a train. It might have been a dream, a nightmare, but that house--there was something about that house. It was calling out to her somehow, drawing her in by revealing each and every minute detail, from the porch swing down to the grain in the hardwood floors where she stared down at her sister's dead body. And now these incredible details of this strange, but familiar, house will now and forever be stained in her mind.

She could feel that her sister was nearby, that she was staying at this old house from her dream. She was positive that she would recognize it in an instant. It was difficult to imagine her sister inside, perhaps unaware that she was being held against her will, and the tragic ending to this vivid nightmare was in her future.

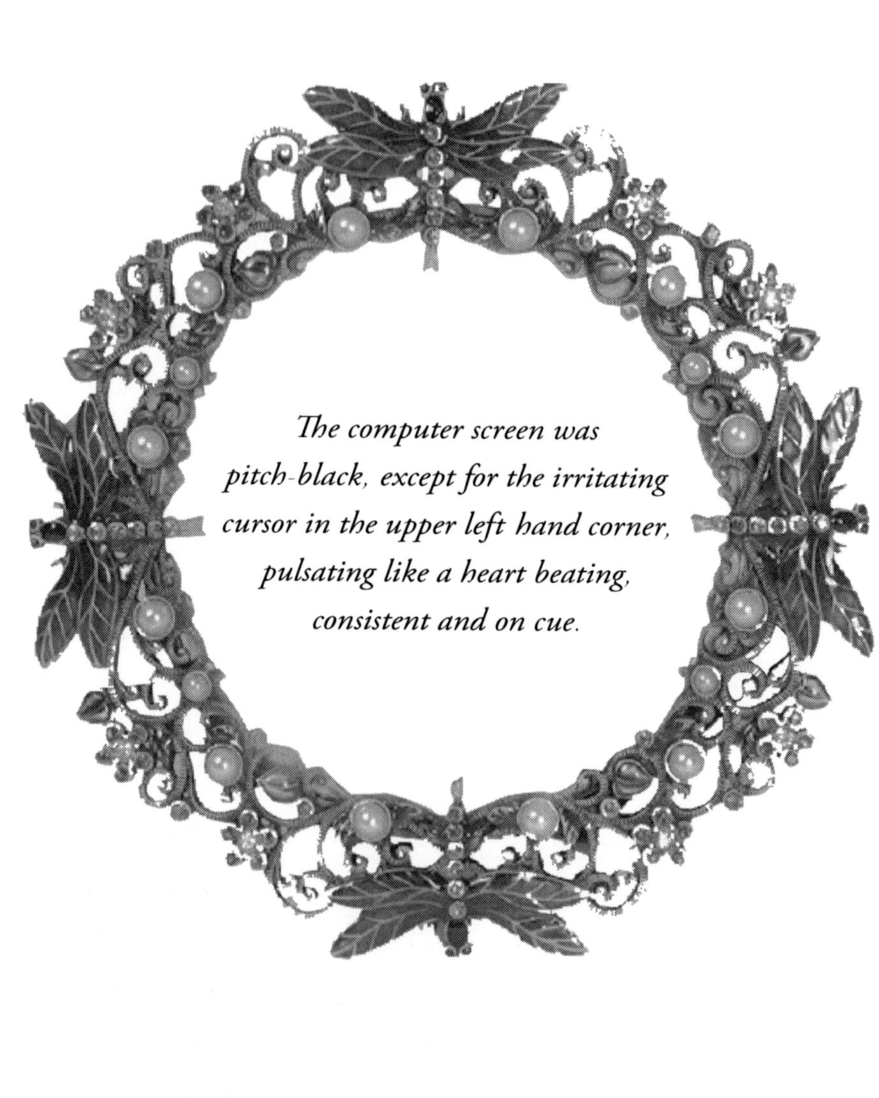

The computer screen was pitch-black, except for the irritating cursor in the upper left hand corner, pulsating like a heart beating, consistent and on cue.

Chapter 20

Between the Lines

Sarah's head never hit the pillow, and soon the night turned into morning. Still in her clothes from the day before, she was pacing the floors in the study, the only room that made her feel safe and secure. Oddly enough, the night was quiet. For the first time in two weeks, she had not encountered any unusual noises coming from inside the walls, or footsteps in the attic. She was convinced now more than ever that this place was haunted and she was not alone, yet she was still in the house. Either she was incredibly brave or incredibly stupid. Getting the hell out would be a much better choice.

She felt conflicted on what she should do now after having the disturbing conversation with Mr. Henesy.

Although he was reluctant at first, her persistence paid off, as he divulged his story, the story she so wanted and needed to hear.

"Oh my God … what is wrong with me? Why am I still here?" Sarah sat down at her writing desk, surveying the cluttered surface. Her research was still resting next to the computer, untouched and abandoned by its creator. Those familiar wide-ruled spiral notebooks were each filled with the scribbles only she could decipher. Without them, she would be lost.

The computer screen was pitch-black, except for the irritating cursor in the upper left-hand corner, pulsating like a heart beating, consistent and on cue. Sarah sat there and stared at it, mesmerized by this tiny dot begging her to come back and write again.

After riffling through the pile of the assorted colored notebooks, each designated for a specific character in her novel, she randomly chose red. Flipping through her master pages, she recalled the real reason why she was staying inside the haunted walls. Turning to the last page, Sarah discovered unfamiliar handwriting, not complicated, and not hers …

Inscribed between the lines were two words: The Keeper.

By definition, "keeper" meant warden, prison guard who with a watchful eye observes his prisoner with relentless intensity.

Chapter 21

With Relentless Intensity

Sarah stood up from the chair, tossing the notebook on the desk, which knocked the others straight to the floor. Thrown off guard, she stumbled over Dickens, but managed to catch herself before falling.

"Jesus, buddy, must you always be under my feet?"

Dickens groaned and changed positions.

Sarah's eyes fixed on the fallen debris, she now had no doubt that Mr. Henesy was telling the truth about the "it" being The Keeper, and the "it" had now gone too far.

By definition, "keeper" meant warden, prison guard who with a watchful eye observes his prisoner with relentless intensity. What did it want? Why was it so important to leave a trail of puzzling clues that she was not able to figure out?

She felt compelled to open the red notebook again and turned to the last page, where the intruder's writing appeared. Each letter was written in a strange format, broken up, separated so it was now obvious that it was three words, not two. "The Keeper" was meant to be read as "The Keep Her."

Holy crap, I am "its" prisoner. I am "Her."

The air became frigid in an instant, and Sarah felt a sensation on her body that was beyond what was on earth. Not quite sure how to react, she stood as still as possible, waiting for whatever it was to pass over her body. Straining her eyes, she could make out what appeared to be impressions of hands skimming the surface of her legs, gliding over her arms, and then pausing on her shoulders. There was no weight to this feeling, yet it felt heavy. The cold penetrated her clothes down to her skin. She prepared herself for its next move, but as sudden as it presented itself, the sensation lifted, not only from her body, but from the room.

"Don't worry; it's gone for now."

"Who's there? Who said that? Show yourself, damn it."

Sarah spun herself around, searching the room, her emotions out of control, and she became physically ill.

"Who are you?" she screamed at the top of her lungs,

her hands holding on to her stomach.

Sarah was not expecting an answer from thin air, but the faint voice returned. "I know where The Keeper hides."

The light in Sarah's eyes darkened, and her posture straightened as the entity slowly consumed her.

Chapter 22

An Unexpected Interruption

Sarah ran out of the study, down the corridor, and into the bathroom. Panic-stricken, she staggered into the shower, not even bothering to take off her clothes. She turned on the hot faucet, and the steam filled the room in an instant. Washing away the disgusting residue from whatever it was that violated her body seemed like the logical thing to do. Her legs became weak, and she found herself sinking fast to the white ceramic tile floor of the shower stall. Resting her head between her knees, she rocked herself back and forth to soothe her nerves.

The doorbell rang out of the blue--not once, but over and over again. Dickens was barking his head off, and this unexpected interruption brought Sarah back to a semi-conscious state. Whoever was on the other side of the door seemed desperate to get inside.

Turning off the faucet, she listened hard and long, thinking there might be a voice that accompanied the irritating sound of the doorbell. Dickens was still barking. She shushed him from behind the bathroom door and stepped out of the shower, and then removed her wet clothes. Thankful her robe was still where she had left it, she put it on over her quivering, wet body.

When she opened the front door and stepped out on the porch, it was clear that whoever was ringing the bell had now gone. The air was stagnant, and by the looks of the dark clouds in the distance, a storm was brewing. Sarah walked from one end of the porch to the other, the thunder rumbling above her, and she called out, "Is anyone there?" There was no answer, but what she did discover was someone's black Jeep parked at the end of the driveway. Convinced now that there was someone prowling around the house, she called out again, "Is anyone there?"

She could hear heavy footsteps walking along the side of the house, and now this person made himself known, by clearing his throat first and then stepping on the walkway. He stood in a stance of authority, his arms crossed, and blurted out his words: "What the hell are you doing here?"

"I should be asking you that question, as you are the one lurking around the property."

"Didn't you see the sign from the road? You can't miss it, I promise."

"Yes, of course I saw the sign; that's how I found this place, by following the sign." Sarah tucked her wet hair behind her ears, her hands still shaking from her incident in the study.

He uncrossed his arms and adjusted his shades.

"You saw the sign that specified that this place is closed and condemned, and under the law of the state of Maine, trespassers will be prosecuted? You saw that sign, right?"

Sarah stared blankly at the officer, trying to process what he was saying to her.

He continued: "I am thinking you didn't see it, which clearly makes you a trespasser on condemned property."

Sarah studied his familiar face and then put it together on why it looked familiar.

"Officer Storms, right?"

"Yes, that's right. I am Riley Storms … and you are?"

"My name is Sarah. We met at the restaurant up the road. I'm a writer, Chicago Bears fan, told you I was staying at a B and B on the hill."

"Oh, that's right, my apologies. I didn't recognize you

at first, but now I do, of course. But I thought for sure you were mistaken on which inn on the hill."

"Were you just ringing the doorbell, officer?"

"No, I haven't set one foot on the porch. I have only had a chance to walk around to the side of the property, and then I heard your voice."

"But the doorbell was ringing, I swear; even my dog heard it."

Sarah looked away from the officer at the door, and it was plain to see there wasn't a button on either side that resembled a bell. "This is insane."

"What are you talking about? What's insane?"

"I heard a doorbell. I know I did, and now I am convinced that this house is making me go crazy. I am losing my mind." Sarah was mumbling her words, her body unsteady and swaying.

"Are you okay, Sarah? You look as if you are going to pass out."

"Actually, no, I am not okay."

"Maybe you should sit on the steps," he said with empathy in his voice.

Sarah took his advice and sat on the top step, her hands resting on her knees.

"I need to understand first of all how you managed to get inside? The reason I am so curious is because the doors and windows have been boarded up and nailed shut for the many reasons I cannot even get into right now. I can say this with confidence because I provided the nails. So, my obvious questions would be, 'Does this place look livable to you?' and, 'Can you see that it is falling apart?' You don't belong here; nobody can stay at The Otter Cove Inn. It has been shut down for good; I told you that back at the restaurant."

"So, let me get this straight. You are telling me right here, right now that this old house has been condemned? Then my obvious assumption is that I must be hallucinating. My supposed clear and concise reasoning would be that I have been a guest here for almost four weeks now. Perhaps this conversation we are having is all part of the illusion I have been living. Are you real, officer? Because I am not even sure I am talking to you at this point."

Sarah asked the question with pure sarcasm, but did not wait for his answer.

"When I checked in this place, it was impeccable and still is. You can see it with your own eyes. Look at it."

"I am looking at it, and it is plain to see from my eyes that it is in complete shambles," Riley insisted.

Sarah started to feel faint and sick to her stomach. Her words were now beyond hysterical.

"But I don't understand. When I arrived, the windows

were not boarded shut, and everything was in its place, from the bone china to the fine art. Officer, you are mistaken and obviously lying right to my face."

"Was there anyone here to check you in, Sarah?"

"No. The front door was unlocked, and so I walked right inside, and the key was …." Her words drifted just as the wind started to pick up. The storm had now moved onshore. The crackling of the lightning settled directly above the house, and the electrical pulses sizzled through the telephone wires.

"Sarah, I am going to say something to you, and I want you to listen first and do not interrupt me. Let me talk, okay? You need to trust me." His voice was serious and monotone. He held up both hands, giving her the signal to hold on a minute.

Sarah pushed herself up from the steps and prepared herself for what he was about to say.

"Turn around and go inside, pack up your stuff, and come with me. Don't ask any questions; just do it. Do it now. Do you hear what I am saying to you?"

The light in Sarah's eyes darkened, and her posture straightened as the entity slowly consumed her. She backed away from Riley, and it was then she realized that no one could save her, that it was now too late.

Riley could see the change in her demeanor and stood

there, his body frozen with the overwhelming feeling of terror, despair, and the complete helplessness of what he was witnessing.

"I am not going anywhere with you. I will leave when I am ready to leave. Do you think I am stupid? Do you think I don't know what is happening to me inside this old house? I know it has control over me. I know what it wants. It wants a new soul, my soul. This is The Keeper's only way of survival, until it drains the life out of each guest and waits for the next to arrive, holding in his hands a personal invitation. I am prepared and willing to give it what it wants; I have no choice, as I am the only guest."

The chairs on the porch were now rocking back and forth, banging up against each other and then rising up off the wooden planks, shaking and out of control. The wind and rain now swirled around her, sending the front door wide open. Sarah's body lifted up off the porch, and she was sucked inside. The door slammed shut.

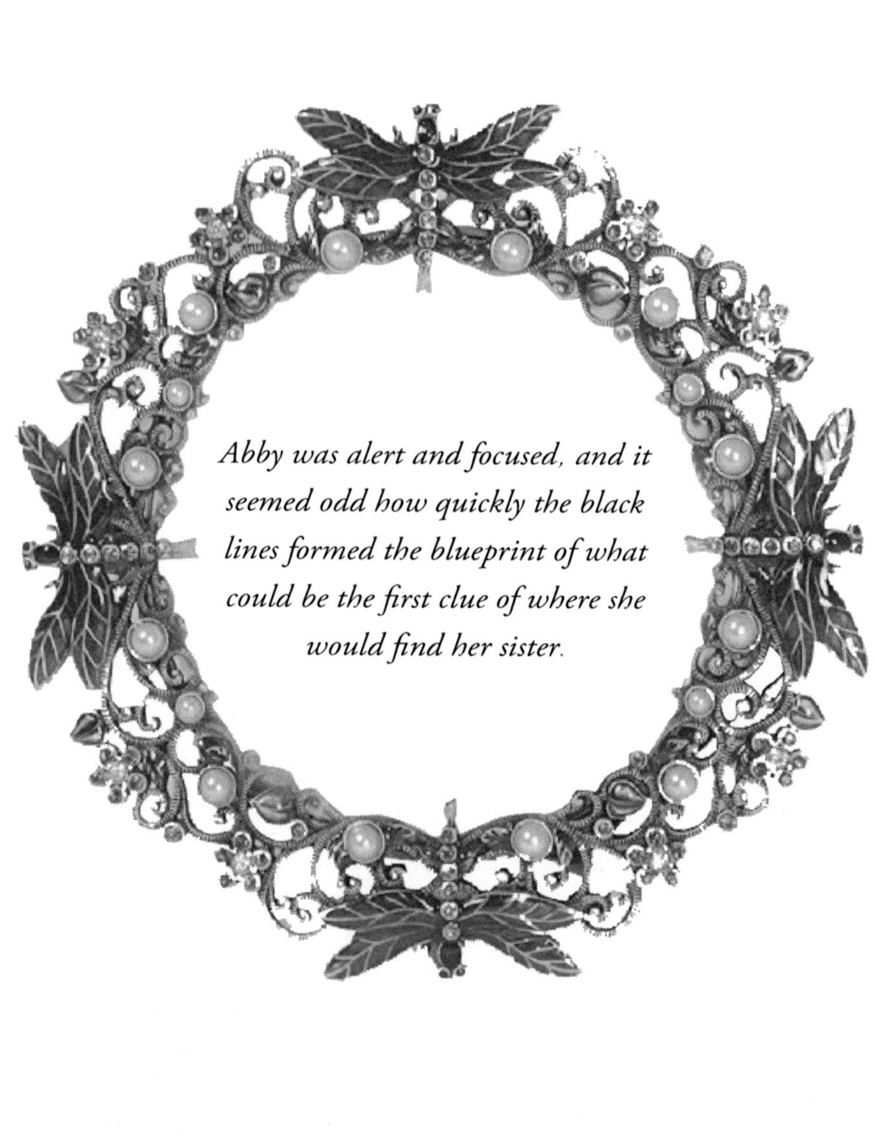

Abby was alert and focused, and it seemed odd how quickly the black lines formed the blueprint of what could be the first clue of where she would find her sister.

Chapter 23

A Haunting Blueprint

As it was not quite 9 A.M., Abby decided to let Tessa sleep in for a while. She couldn't get the nightmare out of her mind and wanted to put the haunting image of the house onto paper before it vanished from her memory. Sliding her sketchpad out of its case, she sat down at the small, round table by the window. Her fingers drummed the clean white canvas in anticipation of filling every inch. As soon as the tip of the charcoal pencil kissed the paper, there was no stopping the artist that held it. Abby was alert and focused, and it seemed odd how quickly the black lines formed the blueprint of what could be the first clue of where she would find her sister. It was all so familiar, from the peak of the roof to the crisscross pattern of the painted lattice under the porch. Never having seen this house before, it came to fruition as if she had lived inside it for her entire life.

It was almost noon by the time Abby finished the drawing. Tessa was now awake and in her own little world, busy talking and singing to her teddy bear. Abby held the sketchpad up in front of her to scrutinize her masterpiece in full spectrum. She surprised even herself, as it turned out exactly how she remembered it from her dream. She stared at it for the longest time, studying the fine details, including the intricate design of the stained glass of the attic window. She couldn't help but wonder if there was some type of meaning behind it, as it was nothing she had ever seen before until now.

"What did you draw, Mommy?" Tessa sat up on the bed, still under the covers, and bounced Teddy up and down on her lap.

Abby looked away from her drawing for a split second to acknowledge her daughter.

"Good morning, my sweet girl, or should I say good afternoon? Did you sleep well?" Turning the sketchpad over, she laid it on the table, avoiding her daughter's question for the moment.

"Yep, I did sleep well, and so did Teddy."

"Well, I am happy for you both. What do you think about going on an adventure with Mommy today?"

"Sure. Can I bring Teddy?"

"Of course, silly. Teddy is a package deal; he goes where you go, right?" Abby leaned in and gave Tessa a squeeze.

"Mommy laid out your clothes in the bathroom, so run and get dressed; go on.... Then it's my turn, so don't dawdle, okay?"

"Okay, Mommy." Tessa climbed out of bed, skipped into the bathroom, and shut the door behind her.

Between the two of them, they were dressed and downstairs in less than thirty minutes. The lobby was full of activity, guests coming and going, families sitting around, sipping coffee and making big plans for the afternoon.

Abby stood behind a young couple at the front desk, waiting her turn to talk with Mr. Cooper. Tessa by her side, to pass the time, she checked out the old pictures that were hanging on the wall behind the desk. For some reason or another, they didn't stand out yesterday, but then again, she was tired and distraught and didn't take notice. There were six pictures, each displayed vertically, descending from the largest to the smallest. The simple black frames embraced what appeared to be old storefronts, bed-and-breakfasts, and antique cars. Abby's eyes traveled from the top picture straight down until she reached the second from the bottom, and her heart stopped. Her sketchpad in one hand, she set her purse down on the floor and anxiously flipped open to the page with her drawing of the inn.

"Tessa, grab my purse, and come with me," Abby snapped.

Together they excused themselves and barged in behind the counter so Abby could see the picture close up, not giving it any thought that they were intruding in a private space.

"I'm sorry, can I help you with something?" Mr. Cooper asked.

Abby slammed the sketchpad up against the wall, shifted her eyes back and forth from the photo to the sketch, comparing the two. Her face was flush, and her teeth were clenched.

"Where is this old house? I have this sick feeling in my stomach that it is close by. Tell me my assumption is correct. I need to go to this place, right now! Do you hear me? Right now!" Abby screamed her questions at the top of her lungs, demanding instant answers.

Clinging to her mommy's leg, Tessa stood in silence, trying to understand what was happening.

"Please calm down, miss; some of the guests are staring."

"I don't care if they are staring."

"To answer your question, Mrs. Grey, Yes, I know where this old house is, but why are you so upset about it?"

"No 'why' questions, if you don't mind; just the directions will suffice."

"Let's step away from the desk so the other guests can't hear us."

Mr. Cooper walked over by the window, and Abby reluctantly followed.

"The Otter Cove Inn is about a forty-minute drive from here in a small town called Cape Elizabeth. Back in the day, this inn was alive and beautiful. Guests would return year after year to stay in its cozy surroundings. It has been closed now for quite some time, and it's in complete shambles, scheduled to be torn down. It might even be condemned by now, but I'm not sure. Nobody can go inside, nor has anyone had the guts to go inside."

Abby stood still, her body numb. She held on to her drawing, letting it hang down by her side, it almost slipping out of her fingers.

"Can I look at your drawing?" Mr. Cooper said, carefully taking the sketchpad away from Abby. She didn't respond; she just let him have it.

"I don't quite understand; this is the exact replica of the house in the picture. How could you have possibly drawn this house if you have never seen it before?"

Mr. Cooper glanced over at the front desk, saw that there were guests waiting, and excused himself for a few minutes, handing her back the sketchpad.

Patrick spotted the two of them from the top of the stairs, overhearing the conversation, as it echoed throughout the entire lobby. He hurried down the stairs and approached Abby, hoping Mr. Cooper would be a while.

"Hello again. Can I speak to you for a minute?"

"Of course. What is it?"

"I know which inn you are talking about. As a matter of fact, I have someone that you should contact that could maybe take you there. I am not sure if Mr. Cooper would want me to give you his number, but I think for your own safety, you should call this guy first, and don't attempt to go there by yourself; it's too dangerous." Patrick handed her a piece of paper, and Abby quickly slid it in her jeans pocket.

"What is it you and Mr. Cooper are not telling me?"

"While I was doing research for a term paper, I stumbled across many articles written about The Otter Cove Inn. It intrigued me, so I dug a little deeper. There were unsolved murders that took place inside, but it goes way beyond just murders. The evidence that I discovered pointed to paranormal activity. There was something evil that checked in, but never checked out. It has no restrictions, no limits, and its shadow glides from one room to another, oblivious by the truth of its own existence."

"How do you know? Have you seen it?"

"No, but the name of the guy on the paper I just gave to you has. And if I may ask, why is it so important that you go to this old inn, anyway?"

Abby stared right into Patrick's curious eyes and whispered … "My sister's inside."

The translucent bulb swayed back and forth, as if it were examining the room, its haunting glow searching for trespassers, as there was no place to hide from its angry glare.

Chapter 24

Words Left Behind

Sarah lay limp and abandoned on the cold, damp floor of a room that was not recognizable, a room that seemed detached from the rest of the inn. Semiconscious, she pushed herself up and dragged her bruised, weak body across the concrete slab in an effort to rest against the walls that framed the space. The light above her was hanging down from the center of the room by a thin unprotected electrical wire. The translucent bulb swayed back and forth, as if it were examining the room, its haunting glow searching for trespassers, as there was no place to hide from its angry glare. Brushing her straggled hair out of her eyes, she quickly assessed the dingy hole that she now occupied against her will. There were no windows, just a steel door that encased the textured brick walls, showing no mercy, no handle, no way out.

The only sound that penetrated the room was her own heartbeat, echoing in her head. Her vision blurred, she focused on the wall closest to the door. Straining her eyes, she realized there were words scratched in the brick and pieces of paper shoved inside the crevices. It was obvious someone else had been inside this room, someone like her.

After sliding herself over to the wall, she caressed the engraved cries for help and then reached her fingers inside the jagged bricks and pulled out some of the notes that were left behind. Written mostly on old receipts, gum wrappers, and scraps, she read the desperate pleas out loud.

"It came for me in the night. I hid under the bed. I know it will come again tonight. I can't get out; it won't let me out."

"The pounding never stops. Make it stop. Please, someone … anyone, make it stop. Help me."

"Tonight is my last night on earth. I can feel it. It is coming for my soul, so it can keep its strength and survive in this evil place."

"The little girl tried to warn me;
I didn't listen. Why didn't I listen?"

Sarah's adrenaline now pumping hard through her veins, she pulled note upon note, one after the other, out of the wall, realizing for the first time she wasn't alone. There were others, so many others that had been tormented and driven completely insane by this evil monster. She continued reading the scribbled final words of its victims, and in her hands, she cradled one last note, a note that would now make sense and would solve the unsolvable mystery of what happened to Catherine and Andrew Willingsworth. It was written and signed by Andrew himself. She stood up and held it under the light, slowly, meticulously unfolding the creased edges. She whispered the faded words that screamed off the paper. Jacob Walker--The Keeper is Jacob Walker.

The note from Andrew clutched in her hand, she lay there, crying quietly, seemingly waiting her turn, realizing that she had reached the final step of the torment for which she was destined.

Chapter 25

The Keeper's Quarters

Sarah curled up in a fetal position in the center of what she assumed to be The Keeper's quarters, a room that oozed of the cold, damp, pure evil of what she now knows to be Jacob Walker. The note from Andrew clutched in her hand, she lay there, crying quietly, seemingly waiting her turn, realizing that she had reached the final step of the torment for which she was destined. The pounding was getting louder, and she knew somehow that it was time, her time. She wished now more than ever that it would just be done; she wanted just to get it over with, sure there was no hope of escaping.

It felt as if hours had passed by, and she was still in the same position. Sarah's eyes started to drift shut, but she caught herself trying her best to stay awake. Falling asleep is not something she wanted to do, but sleep was rushing in at a rapid pace.

Her thoughts were jumbled together; she was mostly wondering where Dickens was and if her sister really thought she was dead, or if it was just The Keeper playing with her mind. The more she thought about everything that happened, she was convinced it was all an illusion, that the ghostly stranger, the supposed fisherman she met on the sidewalk, had created all of it in an attempt for her to be his next victim. It worked; she was literally sucked into his evil charade and believed every word he said--that Lily was his granddaughter and he was a fisherman by trade and spent his time down on the docks, selling his catch of the day. Hardly, and all this time, it must have been Lily trying to warn her, with the subtle hints she had been leaving behind--the key to the trunk, the music box playing in order to go up in the attic, following her to the newspaper building. It was her desperate warning, and she didn't realize it at the time.

Sarah felt as if someone was watching her, and when she looked out of the corner of her eye, she saw a child's doll sitting in the room, as if it had been there the entire time. She convinced herself she was delusional, hallucinating, her mind playing yet another cruel trick on her, but when she sat up to get a clearer view, it was without a doubt a doll sitting in the room. She somehow recognized this doll to be the one in the painting hanging in the corridor. The little girl that was posing in the picture was holding a doll just like this one--same hair, same outfit, same doll.

"You didn't listen to me, and now you will die, just like the others."

Sarah sat up and spun herself around, searching for the voice, her attention directed back to the doll, but this time, a little girl was holding it in her lap, bouncing it up and down, fluffing her dress, and adjusting her blue satin ribbon.

"Where did you come from? How did you get in here? I didn't see you come in."

"Do you think my dolly is pretty? She has a dress on just like me. My mommy gave her to me for my birthday."

Sarah stood up, backed herself into the corner of the room, and hugged the wall, never taking her eyes off the child.

"Oh my God, it's you. You are Lily Rose. I recognize you from the portrait hanging in the hallway."

Sarah watched her closely, mesmerized by this shadowy form that resembled a child and wanting so desperately to believe what she was seeing was real.

"My name is Lily Rose, and I am nine years old. I just had a birthday," she said, still admiring her baby doll.

"When was your birthday, Lily Rose?"

"September 3rd."

"What year?"

"September 3rd, 1818."

Lily Rose stood up, holding her doll tight in her arms, and then twisted and turned so her dress would twirl.

"He is coming for you. He is getting closer.... I can hear him. It is time for me to go. It is time for you to die."

Abby cranked the ignition several more times, twisting the key, forcing the engine to comply with her demands to no avail. It eventually had no more to give, choked, and died in her hands.

Chapter 26

When the Dust Settles

Abby staggered out of the St. John's bed-and-breakfast in a state of shock, bewildered by both her discovery and confirmed intuition about her sister's whereabouts. Although now she had some proof in her hands, she still needed to find the inn and get her sister out of there before it was too late.

Tessa, running alongside her mommy, tried to keep up with her fast pace and long legs.

"What's happening?" Tessa pleaded.

Abby struggled to hunt for her keys, all the while juggling her sketchpad and directions from Mr. Cooper.

"I hear you, Tessa, and I will explain when we get on the road. Now let me gather my thoughts first, okay, sweet girl?"

Abby found her keys in the side pocket of her oversized bag, pressed the unlock button twice, and opened the door for Tessa. Without having to be asked, she climbed in her seat and buckled herself in.

Abby pulled the small piece of paper out of her pocket and keyed the number into her cell so she would be ready to call this person, her supposed savior. Patrick didn't mention his name, but he did say that the number was his cell.

Abby checked the directions first and then pulled out of the parking lot, heading east on Congress Street back toward the highway.

"Okay, Tessa, I know you are wondering what is going on, and to tell you the truth, so am I, but what I can say to you is that we are here for one reason and one reason only. I know you can be a big girl when I tell you this news, so here it goes. We traveled to Portland to look for your Aunt Sarah. I haven't been able to get in touch with her for quite some time, and I am worried about her. I am worried that she could be hurt or sick and she needs our help. So now, Mommy needs your help. Can you do that for me, Tes? We can find her together, what do you say?"

Tessa looked at her mommy's eyes peering back at her in the rearview mirror, pondered the question for about ten seconds, and calmly gave her a simple answer.

"Why didn't you say so in the first place, Mommy? Of course I can help you."

Abby is never surprised at her daughter's maturity and sometimes forgets she is only six years old.

"Thanks, Tessa. We are on our way to the inn where I think she is staying--it isn't too far from here--okay?"

"Okay."

It had been about twenty minutes since they left the parking lot of St. John's, and not one single word was spoken between the two of them. Instead, they gazed out the window at the peaceful scenery that surrounded them, thinking, searching, and hoping they would find Sarah.

Abby was gearing up the courage to call the number already programmed in her phone. She just needed to press the send button, that's all; just hit send. Not quite sure how this nameless stranger would react when she shared her story, her nightmare, the sketch she drew that just so happened to be an identical match to the inn in the photograph couldn't be further from believable. But she was feeling optimistic and ready to pour her heart and soul out to this person for her sister's well-being.

It took just two rings to connect their voices, and the conversation began with a brief introduction from Abby. It was obvious she was talking too fast, not just due to nerves, but due to the dire need to get her words out into the open so the nightmare would stop replaying in her mind like a scene from a horror movie.

On the other end, the voice simply replied, "I will meet you there in fifteen minutes."

"Well, that was a quick conversation," Abby said out loud.

"Who were you talking to, Mommy?"

"The person that is going to help us find your Aunt Sarah. He said his name was Riley and he would meet us in fifteen minutes. He said we were on the right road, and it will lead us to the gravel driveway to The Otter Cove Inn, just up this hill. His instructions were short and to the point, and we were to wait for him there and not attempt to approach the house by ourselves, until he arrived. He didn't even ask me any questions." Abby mumbled a few things to herself so Tessa wouldn't hear.

"Mommy, watch out for that little girl!"

Abby, reacting to her daughter's frightful scream, slammed on the brakes, sending the truck tires skidding across the pavement. Their vehicle was out of control for what seemed like several minutes until coming to its final resting spot, just inches from hitting a tree. A murky cloud of dust kicked up from the road swirled around the truck, and then the engine stalled.

"Oh my God, Tessa. You scared the crap out of me.

What little girl?"

Abby's knuckles were now white from the tight grip on the steering wheel. Once the dust settled, Abby spun around in her seat, checking the perimeter of the truck.

"Tessa, I don't see a little girl. I don't see anyone."

Tessa was now on the verge of tears.

"But there was a girl standing in the middle of the road. I saw her with my own eyes, Mommy, I did."

"I am sure you just thought you saw a little girl."

While trying to convince Tessa it was only her imagination, Abby cranked the ignition several more times, twisting the key, forcing the engine to comply with her demands to no avail. It eventually had no more to give, choked, and died in her hands. Pounding her fists as hard as she could on the dashboard, she slammed her body back in the seat.

"This is just great. Now what are we going to do?"

"Mommy?"

"What is it, Tessa?"

"The little girl that I saw standing in the road, she is sitting next to me inside the truck."

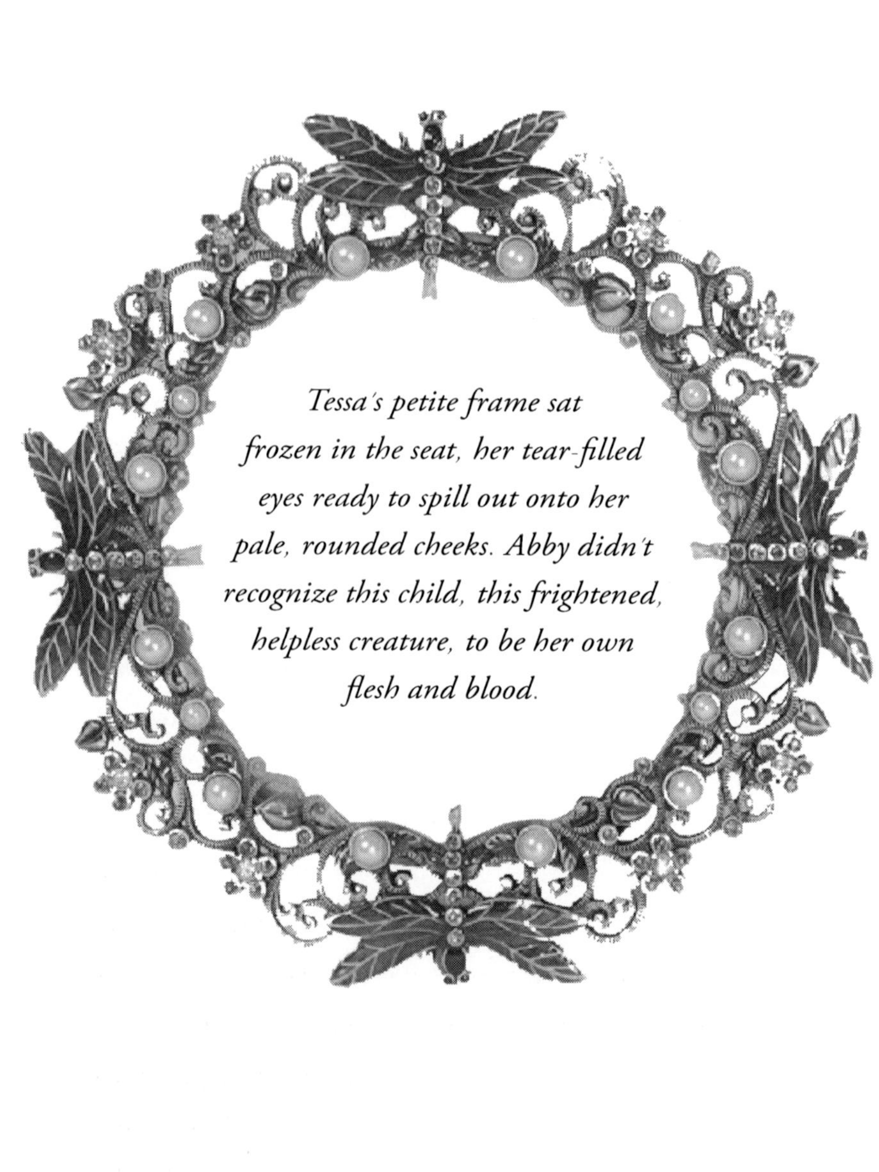

Tessa's petite frame sat frozen in the seat, her tear-filled eyes ready to spill out onto her pale, rounded cheeks. Abby didn't recognize this child, this frightened, helpless creature, to be her own flesh and blood.

Chapter 27

A Child's Whisper

Abby's fists clenched in her lap, she swallowed hard and reluctantly allowed the fear to creep in. Grasping on to her daughter's words of this sudden intrusion made no sense; it made no sense at all. What would a little girl be doing alone on an abandoned road, and how did she get inside the truck without their even knowing it? Convinced that her daughter was just imagining things, she readied herself and turned around.

Tessa's petite frame sat frozen in the seat, her tear-filled eyes ready to spill out onto her pale, rounded cheeks. Abby didn't recognize this child, this frightened, helpless creature, to be her own flesh and blood. By the look on her daughter's face, whatever it was that scared her had to be real in her mind.

"Tessa, sweetie, are you okay?"

"Is the little girl still sitting next to me?"

"No, honey, there is nobody sitting next to you."

"Are you sure?"

"Yes, I'm sure."

Abby reached over the tan upholstered seat to comfort her daughter. As Abby gently placed her hand on top of small, icy fingers, a sudden panic came over her.

"Tessa, you are so cold. I am getting you out of this truck."

Abby opened her door and then Tessa's. Then Abby unbuckled the seat belt and scooped Tessa up in her arms. Together they stood on the side of the road. The temperature was dropping, and there was a mist in the air. Tessa melted into her mother's embrace. Her tiny limbs spilling over her mother's shoulders, she buried her head in the nape of her neck and sobbed.

"Tessa, you're okay; don't cry, sweetie. I know you are upset, and I am so sorry that happened. We are going to have to walk the rest of the way, and I honestly don't think Mommy can carry you."

"No, I want you to carry me, and why can't we ride in the truck?" Tessa said, wiping her tears on her mommy's shirt.

"The truck doesn't work, Tes, so we will need to walk and try to find the driveway that leads to the inn. I will hold on to your hand; you can do it. I have this feeling that the inn is at the top of this hill."

"Fine. You can put me down; I'll walk," Tessa said, realizing she wasn't going to get her way.

Abby set her on the ground and crouched down in front of her, smoothing out her long blonde hair in an attempt to calm her down. Tessa folded her arms and pouted.

"Tessa, I am so sorry you were so scared. Whatever you saw in the road was probably a stray dog or something crossing the street. However, I am not sure what you saw sitting next to you."

Tessa, stomping her foot on the pavement, defended herself. "I saw a little girl. She was standing in the middle of the road, and then she sat right next to me in the truck. Why don't you believe me? She was my size, wearing a dress and black shiny shoes, and holding a doll in her arms. She was real; I know it."

"Oh, Tessa, I so want to believe you. I really do." Abby gave her a kiss on her cheek.

She stood up and opened the truck door, grabbed her purse, their jackets, and Tessa's bear, and then slammed it shut and locked it.

"Let's start walking. Maybe Riley will spot us and give us a ride. Here's your bear, sweetie, and let me help you with your jacket." Abby put on Tessa's jacket and then adjusted the pale lavender collar.

"Mommy, I need to tell you something."

"What is it, Tes? You can tell me anything; you know that."

"She whispered something to me."

"Who whispered something to you?"

"The little girl; she said something to me when she was in the truck."

"What did she say?"

"She said, 'It's too late … you can't save her now.'"

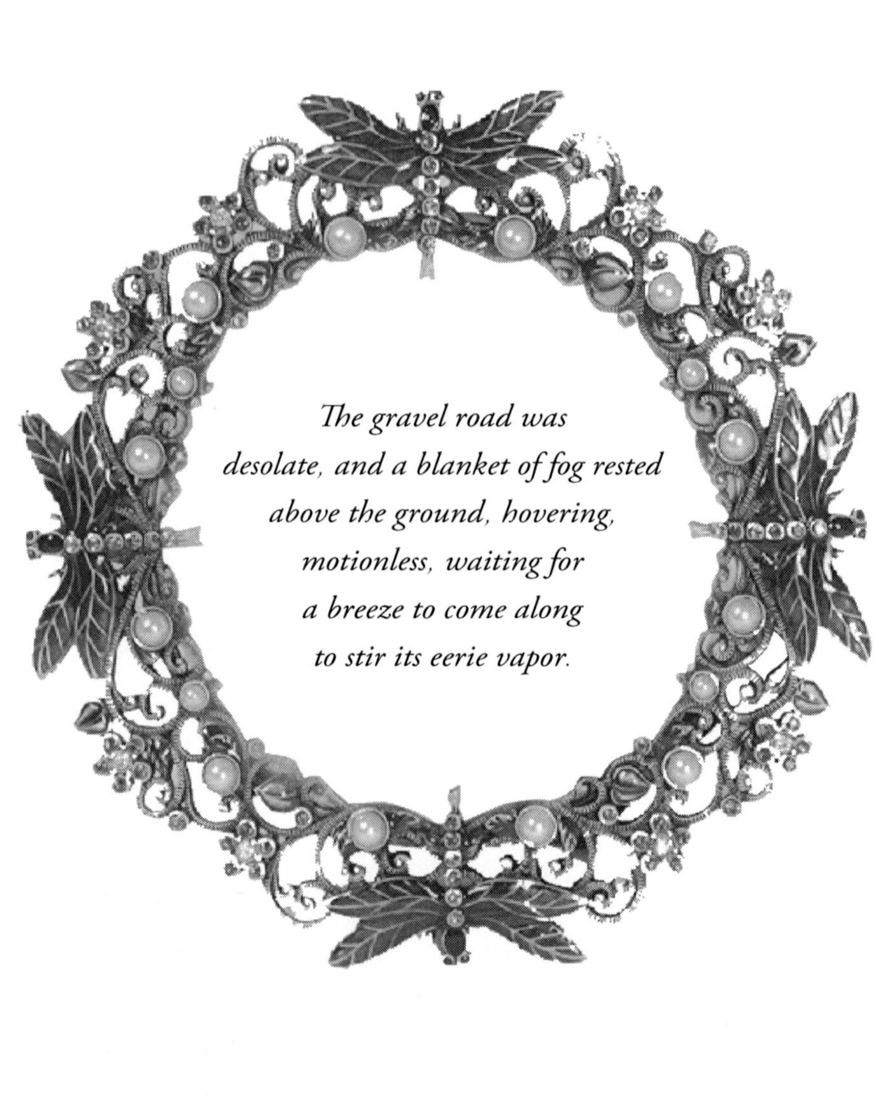

The gravel road was
desolate, and a blanket of fog rested
above the ground, hovering,
motionless, waiting for
a breeze to come along
to stir its eerie vapor.

Chapter 28

The Vine Covered Gate

Side by side, they stood at the entrance of the road that would lead to the old house they had been searching for, the haunting inn that held their loved one captive. As they peered through the vine-covered gate, their fingers clasped onto the prickly surface, giving them a sense of security while they waited for their guide. Chained to the gate hung a weathered sign that sent out a clear message to those who attempted to pass through. The gravel road was desolate, and a blanket of fog rested above the ground, hovering, motionless, waiting for a breeze to come along to stir its eerie vapor. Enormous trees lined both sides, some of them naked of the greenery that used to be, leaving the branches vulnerable to the elements and a foreseeable demise.

Not able to see the house from the gate, Abby could feel the emotions start to take over. She and Tessa had been waiting over forty-five minutes now for this stranger to arrive, unaware of what he was about to share with them, and wondering if he could be trusted. There was something about the tone in his voice that made her think he was hiding the truth about her sister.

"Tessa, I am getting so worried. Where is this guy? I cannot believe I brought you out here. I am so sorry."

As Tessa was staring out into the foggy mist, her eyes were captivated by something in the pathway, something that was making her entire body tremble. Unresponsive to her mother's words, she tried to utter her own.

"Tessa? Did you hear me?"

"Yes, Mommy, I heard you."

"Are you all right?"

"I'm cold."

"I know you are, sweetie," Abby said, rubbing Tessa's arms to help her warm up.

"I'm going to go see if there are any cars coming this way, so I need you to wait right here. Don't move, okay? I won't be far."

Tessa said nothing as her mother walked away, leaving her there shivering, helpless, and now alone. She peered through the small opening in the gate, and glanced over her shoulder to make certain her mother wasn't looking. With a slight push, the one thing that was keeping them from entering had now unwillingly welcomed her with an eerie quiet. The sharp points on the gate scraped the ground, digging into the rock and soil, clinging to whatever it could to stop this child from going beyond its restricted barrier.

Now standing in the middle of the hazy gloom, Tessa kept a watchful eye on the shadows that danced between the trees. The haunting house was now visible, and sitting on the front steps was the little girl that she had come to know. Their eyes met, and her loneliness and gloom radiated directly into Tessa, which made her heart ache for her mother's embrace.

"I am sad," she whispered.

"Why?"

"I have no one to play with."

Tessa said nothing, as she sensed there was something not right with this little girl. She appeared to be sweet and innocent, but there was something wicked and resentful in her eyes.

"I want you to play with me."

"I cannot; I am waiting for my mommy to come and get me."

"My mother is dead, you know? The Keeper killed her."

Tessa, in shock by what she had said, could see the anger building inside this child and wanted so desperately to run away, but she was frozen in her stance, unable to move in any direction.

"Come with me; we could be sisters."

"No, I don't want to."

"You will come with me; I can make you. The Keeper has his prisoner, and now you will be mine."

Tessa heard a banging sound coming from one of the second-story windows, and when she looked up, she could see a hand pressed up against the glass. The weak, limp fingers lay motionless on the transparent surface and then gradually slid down the window, with nothing to grasp onto. Eventually, the hand vanished, leaving behind a faint, but distinct, outline.

There was nothing Tessa could do. She couldn't stop the girl. She fell silent to her demands, unable to scream out for help, and now it was too late; she was inside the house.

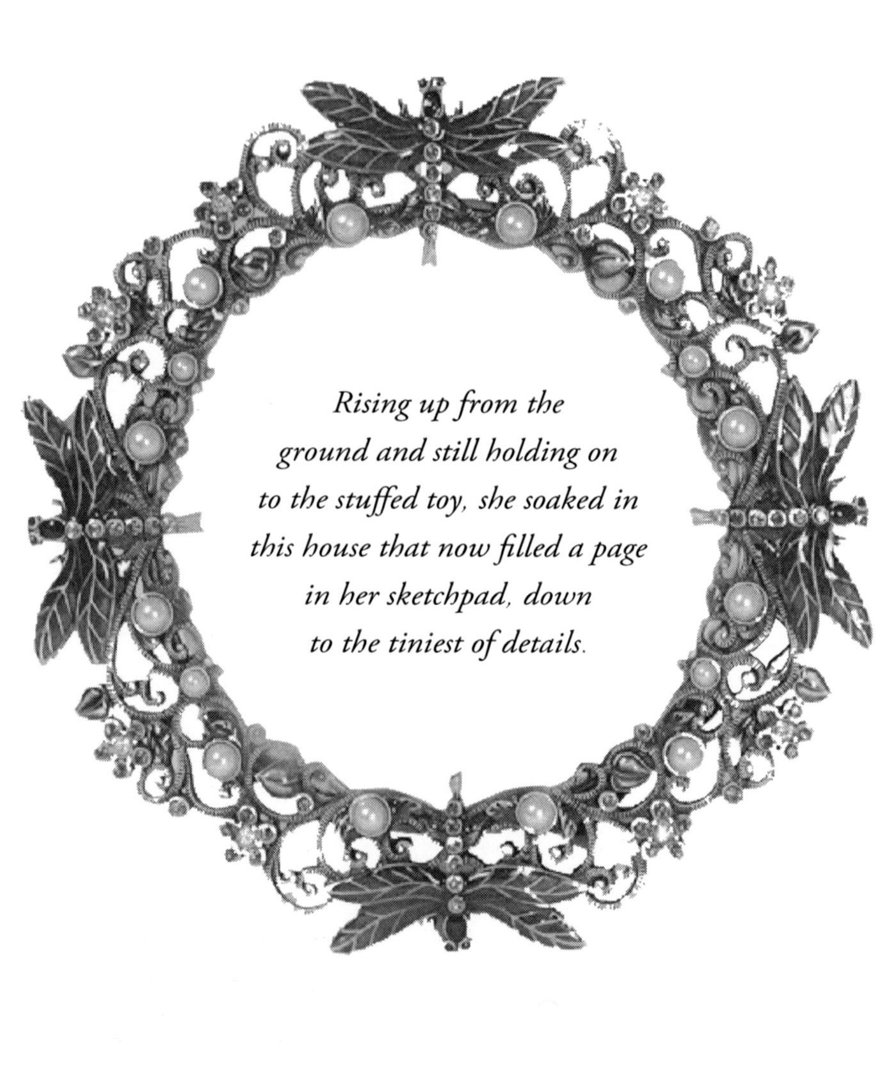

Rising up from the ground and still holding on to the stuffed toy, she soaked in this house that now filled a page in her sketchpad, down to the tiniest of details.

Chapter 29

A Carbon Copy

Abby knelt on the ground in front of the inn, clutching in her arms her daughter's stuffed companion. It was then she realized that it was the single, solitary visible evidence that her little girl was standing in front of this broken-down dwelling just moments ago. She had to have struggled and put up a tremendous fight, as she would never let go of her teddy bear. Someone must have taken her inside the house. Abby was punishing herself for leaving Tessa in such a terrible place for even those few minutes. The anger now grew to enormous measures for the faceless stranger, Riley, who did not keep his word.

Rising up from the ground and still holding on to the stuffed toy, she soaked in this house that now filled a page in her sketchpad, down to the tiniest of details. The one thing that was missing, completely left out of the picture, was in reality--the house was in shambles, boarded up and abandoned.

Abby studied the exterior for several minutes, putting herself in somewhat of a trance thinking about what her plan should be to get inside and search for her sister and now her daughter. While Abby was oblivious to any sounds around her, someone interrupted her deep concentration.

"You know, when you intentionally cross the threshold into an environment where you are certain there is an entity waiting for its next victim, you should prepare yourself to feel."

Abby stayed in the exact position, and for some reason, this voice behind her didn't startle her; expecting to lash out harshly, she responded with strength and control.

"I don't know who you think you are, but that is not something that you should say to someone that cannot find her six-year-old daughter or her sister, for that matter. If you were trying to be funny, it didn't amuse me, and if you are trying to make up for being so freaking late, that didn't work, either. Now, because of you, my daughter is inside this horrific place."

"I apologize for my being so late, I really do. But I am here now, so let's figure this out together; I am all you got. I'm Riley, by the way; you must be Abby."

"What do you mean, you are all I got?"

"I couldn't get anyone to come with me to help. No one believed me, and to tell you the truth, after what I saw with my own eyes less than twenty-four hours ago, I don't even believe me. But the real honest-to-God truth is that the people that know about this inn are scared out of their minds and will not under any circumstances come within fifty feet of this place. And that is one of the reasons why it is still standing. All the people of Cape Elizabeth turned their backs on the truth, and most just pretend like nothing has ever happened inside these ghostly walls. So, again, I am all you got, and I will help you get your sister and now daughter out of this godforsaken hellhole."

"My sister is inside, isn't she?"

"Yes, she is."

"How do you know for sure?"

"I was brought here by something I cannot explain. I didn't come here by choice, and that's a promise. I had a dream or a vision, not sure what to call it, but in my dream, I saw a young woman inside this house, and she was in immense danger. I couldn't make out her face, but she was trapped inside, desperate to get out. So, I drove out here to see for myself if I was losing it or if it was true somehow. When I arrived, the inn looked the same, just how I remembered it. It was just last year that I volunteered to come out here alone and board the place up. I brought in truckloads of plywood and covered up every window, every door, even the chimney. I used what seemed like hundreds of nails, pounded them hard into blue clapboard, and sealed it up tight. I posted a no trespassing sign and roped it across the porch. It seemed logical; if I closed this place up tight and nailed it shut, nothing could get in, and nothing could get out. I was wrong."

"What do you mean, nothing could get out?"

"Let me finish, please."

Abby shifted her weight, feeling uneasy and anxious.

"I heard a voice call out while I was walking the perimeter of the house. It scared me, so I ran in the direction it was coming from. Standing on the porch was a young woman with the same demeanor, same hair color as the woman in my dream. When I looked at her close up, I realized it was Sarah, Sarah Reddington, the writer, your sister. I had met her at one of the local restaurants the week before. She was calling out and asking if anyone was there, and it should have been me asking her that question. I pleaded with her over and over that she did not belong in this horrible place. I told her that it was not livable or safe and she should pack up and come with me, trying hard not to give her the real reason why she should get out of the house. She argued with me and tried to convince me that she had been staying here as a guest and didn't see that the inn was falling apart, and called me a liar right to my face. I saw her with my own eyes and spoke with her for several minutes before *it took her.*"

"It *took her?*"

"Yes, it took her. One minute she was standing on the porch, and then the next, something came for her; a powerful force picked her up and sucked her inside the house. It happened so fast, I had no time to react. It was the most unbelievable, frightening thing I have ever witnessed in my life. It was then that I realized, the vision, the dream, the nightmare I had just days before was a carbon copy. I tried for hours to get inside … it wouldn't let me in."

Together they stood on
the porch, drowning in their
unspoken thoughts as the fear rushed
in and confronted
them face to face.

Chapter 30

Haunting Cries

Abby ran up the porch steps, and her fists beat on the splintered wood that covered the front door. She screamed hysterically, and it felt as though her lungs would burst. She didn't recognize the sound of her own voice.

"Tessa, Sarah, open the door; if you can hear me, open the door."

Riley grabbed her wrist.

"Abby, they can't hear you. They are not anywhere near the door."

"Don't you think I know that?"

Abby jerked her hand away, the tears streaming down her face.

"I can't just stand here; I have to do something. My baby girl is inside this broken-down house, and I have to get to her somehow."

"There is a way. We will find it, I promise."

"Riley, look at me. Can't you see what's happening? Don't you realize by now? We were both brought here by pure evil, the immortality that we allowed ourselves to surrender to in our vision. You said you had to question if your vision was a nightmare. Isn't it obvious now that you are here and in the moment? I don't have to question mine, because it was a nightmare. If your dream played back exactly how you dreamt it, then my nightmare will do the same. I saw my sister inside this house; I saw what happened to her with my own eyes. I keep playing it back in my head over and over again, the same image of her broken body falling down the stairs and there isn't a damn thing I can do about it. If I can somehow get inside, I could stop it from happening, stop it from coming true."

"Abby, I know that whatever is inside this house has the control, the control over whatever and whomever it summons, as it holds the key."

Together they stood on the porch, drowning in their unspoken thoughts as the fear rushed in and confronted them face to face. The windows buried under the layers of plywood began to rattle, and a pounding noise seeped through the cracks and crevices, echoing all around them. The rusty nails twisted and turned, and then ejected themselves out with a violent force, sending the metal pins flying like missiles past the uninvited guests. The boards that were once adhered to the casement surrendered and crashed hard to the ground.

Abby and Riley crouched down and took cover from this unexplained phenomenon. The front door was now visible, and the brass handle ready to turn; resting in the keyhole, the key.

"Could it be that simple?" Riley asked, heaving the debris away from the door to clear the way.

"Is this really happening?" Abby asked, trying to come to grips with what she was witnessing.

"It knows we're here."

Abby turned the key, and the connection was abrupt and deliberate. Her hands shaking, she tapped on the door lightly, the hinges rotating on contact, allowing access to the inside.

With guarded hesitation, they stepped inside the entryway, now vulnerable to the haunting cries that surrounded them. The scene resembling her nightmare, Abby took the same path that would lead her to the familiar staircase, preparing herself for the worst.

Sitting at the bottom of the stairs was not what she was expecting. It was Dickens. He didn't acknowledge their presence or even bark. His back was to them, and his eyes were staring straight up to the top floor.

"Dickens, come here, boy."

"You know this dog?"

"He's my sister's dog, and he is acting as if he doesn't even see us."

Abby and Riley looked up the steep staircase beyond the first level, straining to see whatever it was that Dickens was looking at.

"I knew you would come for her, and now you have made The Keeper angry."

The faint voice made itself known when its shadowy figure crawled out from behind the dark spindles of the banister. It was a little girl, the same little girl that Tessa encountered. Her frightening description was one hundred percent accurate, from the dress she was wearing down to her black patent leather shoes. The ghostly child sat herself at the top step, placed her feet together, and folded her hands in her lap.

Sitting to her side was a music box. She reached over to it, opened the lid, and it played a haunting tune.

"The music will calm him down; it always does."

Abby climbed the rickety steps, approaching the spirit, keeping her voice soft in an attempt to earn her trust.

"Please, I beg of you, tell me where my daughter and sister are, and then we will leave you alone."

The music only played louder, and the staircase started to shake and sway out from underneath her feet. Acting quickly, Riley stepped up on the steps and pulled Abby back to the floor level to keep her from falling through the cracks.

The plaster from the ceiling was crumbling, and the walls were caving in. The house had fallen to its mercy and was now surrendering to its will. It was clear the entity did not want them there and would do anything to keep them away from the dreadful fate he had planned for his imprisoned victims.

"He is coming!" was the desperate and last warning from the little girl, and then she disappeared back into the shadows.

A loud, piercing, high-pitched cry for help came from the third floor. Riley and Abby quickly made their way up the broken-down staircase, only to discover complete and total chaos. The doors were flying open and slamming shut; the crystal handles were turning by themselves, rattling and shaking out of control. They searched each room, calling out for Tessa and Sarah, their voices now blending together as one as they chanted their names over and over.

"Mommy!"

"Oh my God, Tessa."

Huddled in the corner of one of the abandoned guest rooms was her frightened daughter. Her body trembling, her face pale, she reached out for her mother's embrace, in shock and not able to utter a word. Abby scooped her up and carried her into the hallway, only to find Riley mesmerized by the woman standing on the edge of what was left of the staircase. She didn't look real. Abby called out her sister's name. She didn't respond. She just stood there, her body wavering, teetering between solid ground and midair. She took one look at Abby and threw herself off the platform.

The medics arrived within a short time and lifted her sister's body onto the stretcher and then into the ambulance. The oxygen mask was covering her face and pumping life back into her weak, collapsed lungs.

There was not much left of the house that was once

known as The Otter Cove Inn, just its empty shell--although a dim light illuminated from the attic window and standing in the shadows was a little girl, clutching her doll. There she waits for "The Keeper" to summon his next guest so she can give her warning with her haunting cries.

Adjusting her collar and fidgeting with her hair, she nervously waited for the moment, her moment to present her masterpiece.

Epilogue

Six weeks later …

The elevator glided from the ground level to the top floor of Maple Leaf Publishing without interruption. The doors opened to the main reception area, leading to the one and only office on the floor, the publisher's. The room was grand and tastefully decorated, down to the finest of details. Hanging above the desk was the most important touch, the Maple Leaf logo, the motif simple, but elegant.

"Hello. She is expecting you. Follow me."

The short walk to Anna's office was as she remembered, and the butterflies started turning in her stomach, as always when she reached this point.

"Please, have a seat; Ms. Harrison will be right with you."

The view was magnificent, and now with the added touch of the soft, falling snow, it made it even more incredible.

Adjusting her collar and fidgeting with her hair, she nervously waited for the moment, her moment to present her masterpiece. Her manuscript was finally done. After all of these weeks of rewrites, edits, and adjustments, the day had finally arrived that she could present it to her publisher.

Anna breezed into her office with an excitement and enthusiasm Sarah had not seen before and embraced her with a warm welcome back and air kisses for both cheeks.

"Is that it?" Anna said, staring down at the package in Sarah's lap.

"Yes. Here you go; it's all yours," Sarah handed Anna the manila envelope, and she hurriedly opened the brass clasp and pulled out the bound pages.

"Your title, it's surprising, as I was expecting something totally different."

"Yes, I know. Believe me, so was I."

"Why did you title it *The Keeper*?" she asked while adjusting her glasses in preparation to bury herself in her desk chair and start to read.

"Anna, you will have to read every word to find out. Now, it was great to see you, but I need to go and get settled back into my life here in Chicago. I can show myself out."

Stepping onto the elevator, she turned her body toward the panel of buttons, contemplating which one to press.

"I know who you really are, and you will never get away with it, Mr. Walker." The child's voice whispered.

Sarah smiled, pressed the button for the ground floor, and said, "That's what you think."

The doors closed....

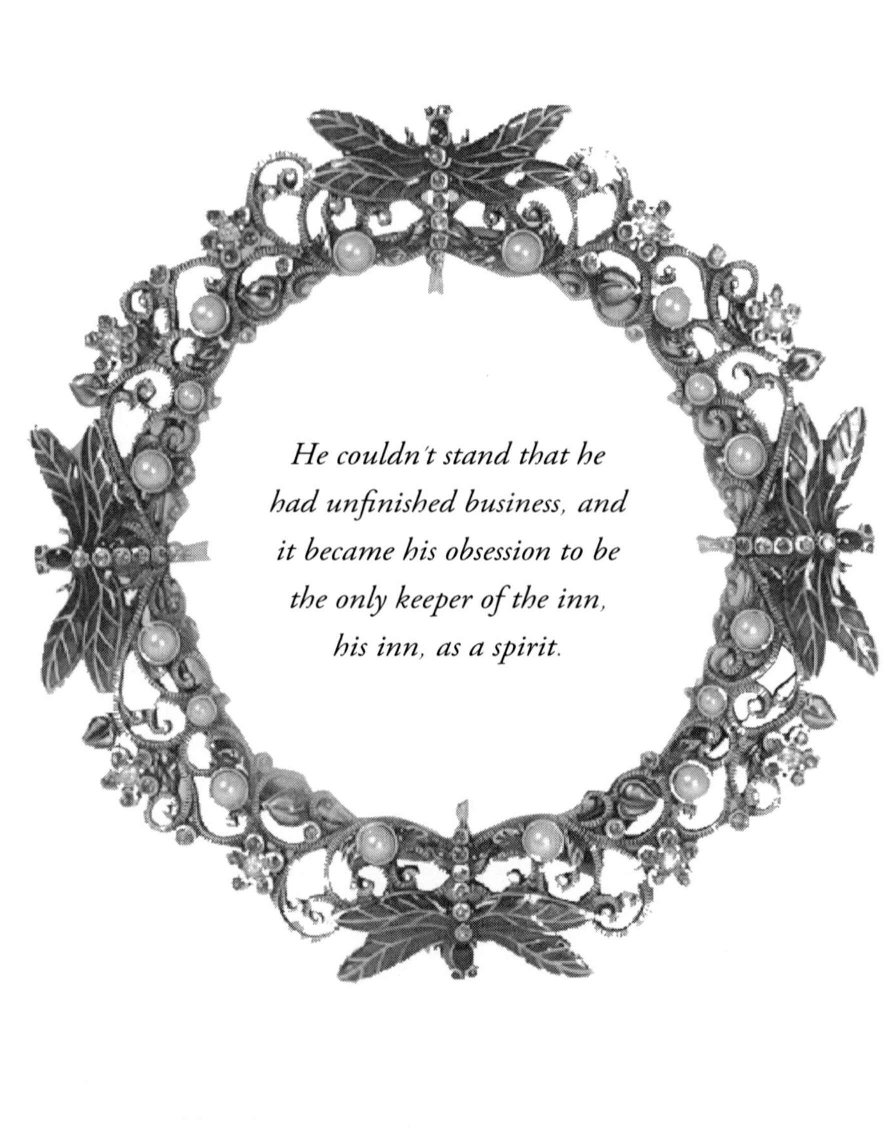

He couldn't stand that he had unfinished business, and it became his obsession to be the only keeper of the inn, his inn, as a spirit.

An Afterthought

The Keeper

Jacob Walker was the owner of The Otter Cove Inn, and Catherine and Andrew Willingsworth offered to buy it from him at a price he could not refuse. After he sold it to them and signed the deed, he had a change of heart and asked for it back. They refused, and they argued and disagreed until finally to appease him, they hired Jacob as the handyman and groundskeeper so he could still be involved somehow. He reluctantly agreed, but had a chip on his shoulder, and became bitter and resentful, and eventually hostile, toward the couple. He didn't agree on the changes that took place at the inn, and there were many disagreements until it got so ugly and he went into a rage and killed them both, leaving their dead bodies on the stairs.

Lily, their daughter, was the only witness, but she too died while running from Jacob and fell off the cliff to her death, her body never to be found. Jacob never reported it and covered up the crime and lied to the police. His alibi stood to be true, as others said they saw him on his boat fishing. That day he had the biggest catch, and the story and his picture ended up in the daily newspaper. He was cleared of all charges. He took the inn back as his own, but soon after, he was killed in a boating accident. He couldn't stand that he had unfinished business, and it became his obsession to be the only keeper of the inn, his inn, as a spirit. The only way he could survive is by pulling people in and taking their souls for his own so he could keep his strength and take care of the inn. The pounding was Jacob's hammering and fixing the place up. Even though it was in shambles, he saw it still alive and beautiful, his pride and joy.

Lily's lost spirit tried to give warning to every guest that was summoned by The Keeper that the place was evil and to stay away, but her haunting cries didn't work for most, and they all ended up in The Keeper's quarters, their prison, until he killed them with his evil strength.

Lightning Source UK Ltd.
Milton Keynes UK
UKOW051212150512

192599UK00001B/9/P